AF489503

The Belle Rive Ledger

A Scales of Justice Novel

C.L. Carmichael

Copyright © 2026 Candis L. Carmichael All rights reserved

The characters and events portrayed in this book are fictitious. Any similarity to real persons, living or dead, is coincidental and not intended by the author.

No part of this book may be reproduced, or stored in a retrieval system, or transmitted in any form or by any means, electronic, mechanical, photocopying, recording, or otherwise, without express written permission of the publisher.

Dedicated to my mother,
who instilled in me a love of reading,
the confidence to follow my dreams and
an unapologetic sprinkling of magic.

And to my dearest Love Dove.
You have been my rock,
my courage, and my staunchest supporter.
Without you, this would never have been possible.

I love you now and always.

Prologue

The Woman in the Garage

Mireille Baptiste leaned against the concrete pillar in the courthouse parking garage, the kind of place where fluorescent lights buzzed like angry wasps and the air always smelled of exhaust and wet asphalt. It was late—past nine, the hour when the building emptied out except for janitors and lawyers who didn't know when to quit. She wasn't waiting for anyone specific. She was waiting for the current.

The hum started low, a vibration in her teeth first, then settling in her chest like a second heartbeat. It wasn't sound. It was pressure, the world tilting just enough to notice. Mireille straightened, eyes scanning the shadows between cars. There third row, battered gray sedan pulling in slow, tires hissing on damp concrete.

The woman who got out was young, sharp-featured, dark hair yanked into a hasty ponytail, navy blazer rumpled from a long day. Camille Durant. Mireille knew the name from her cousin Émiline's basement ledgers. Today's "miracle": first big unwinnable assault case flipped—key evidence vanished overnight from lockup; jury swayed on a chain-of-custody technicality that no one else spotted. Families in the gallery upstairs, faces carved hollow with grief. Mireille had felt it from two blocks away, sharp as river wind.

Camille slammed the car door, slung a battered briefcase over her shoulder, and muttered to the empty air as she walked: "...without that chain of custody, prosecution's got nothing. Clean win."

The current thrummed approval, silver threads weaving tight around her—Émiline's nudges, subtle as a clerk "misplacing" a file. Camille moved like victory agreed with her: stride lengthening, shoulders easing, oblivious to the shadows. She passed Mireille's pillar without a glance, heels clicking sharp against concrete, replaying her closing argument like a victory lap.

Mireille stayed put, breath steady, letting the woman's aura brush past—bright luck, too steady for chance, laced with that faint, off-kilter balance. Promising asset, Émiline had scrawled in the ledger. Not yet aware. Not yet costing.

Camille vanished up the exit ramp, echo fading. The garage lights hummed on. Mireille slipped out into the drizzle, pulling up her hood. Back in her walk-up above the botanica supply shop, she'd light a candle, call Émiline.

"She's hooked," she'd say. "Doesn't question the breaks. Yet."

Outside, New Orleans rain pattered steady, washing the city clean of nothing. The current waited, patient as silt. Camille Durant was marked—one impossible verdict at a time.

Chapter 1

The Summons

The invitation arrived the same day the jury set a killer free.

Camille Durant found it waiting on her kitchen table, lying on a stack of unopened bills and glossy charity mailers like it owned the place. Heavy black stock, silver ink, her name written in a looping hand that looked expensive and old-fashioned, the way people wrote before email and indictments. The envelope had no return address, only a New Orleans postmark and a faint smell of smoke and magnolia blossoms when she slit it open.

She read it standing up, coat still on, the taste of the courthouse air still sour in the back of her throat.

> *Ms. Durant,*
>
> *You are cordially invited to a private weekend at Belle Rive, the historic home of the LeBlanc family, to discuss matters of mutual interest and future collaboration.*
>
> *Your discretion is, as ever, assumed.*
> *— A. LeBlanc*

There was a date—two weeks from Friday—and beneath it, in small, elegant type, a list of "selected attendees": judges, business owners, a state senator, two names she recognized from the environmental scandal that had been eating the local news for months. Near the bottom of the list, in the same neat script, someone had written in a later addition: Mireille Baptiste.

Camille read that name twice, then set the card down carefully, as if it might burn.

The rain had started on her drive home, a thin, needling drizzle that turned the city's lights into smeared halos. By the time she'd parked and climbed the steps to the narrow shotgun house she still called "temporary," the drizzle had sharpened into a steady fall. The back of her blouse stuck to her spine. Her heels had left faint wet crescents on the tile.

On the television in the front room, a news anchor talked brightly over footage of the courthouse steps. Someone—her client, the newly acquitted Mr. Kline—was walking out into the cameras' flashes, his tie straightened, his smile controlled. A chyron at the bottom of the screen crawled:

LOCAL BUSINESSMAN ACQUITTED IN DOUBLE HOMICIDE; FAMILIES "DEVASTATED."

Camille reached for the remote, turned the volume down. The room settled into a murmur of voices and rain.

She picked up the invitation again. Belle Rive. The name tugged at something in her memory—a photo in a magazine, a footnote in a brief. A plantation house turned luxury "heritage venue." Old money dressed up as culture and history. The LeBlancs had been landowners since before anyone wrote down who built their land for them.

Your discretion is, as ever, assumed.

It rolled around in her head with an implied familiarity she did not feel. She had never met the LeBlancs socially; they existed on the periphery of each other's orbit—names on contracts, figures behind campaign donations. Whoever had written that line knew at least one thing about her, though: Camille Durant did not talk out of turn. And she couldn't resist a hint of mystery or intrigue.

Rain pattered harder against the windows. Somewhere down the block, a siren wailed and then faded.

She slipped the invitation back into its envelope and placed it on the counter, away from the bills. Away from her. It did not belong. Nothing about Belle Rive's cursive promises had anything to do with "the usual." It was a misfit. And it oozed with misgivings that unnerved her.

Her phone buzzed. She glanced at the screen: an unknown number, local area code. The courthouse had trained her to answer those. That's exactly how the calls from the courthouse displayed, no matter how many times she tried to program the various numbers from private offices.

"Durant."

A beat of silence, filled with wet static, and then a woman's voice: low, unhurried, carrying something like a smile.

"Ms. Durant," the voice said. "I see you've received your summons."

Camille's fingers tightened around the phone and her voice caught in her throat for a heartbeat. "My summons? Who is this?" she asked curtly.

"A mutual acquaintance," the woman replied. "Of yours and Madame LeBlanc's. I merely wished to ensure it was clear: this is not the kind of invitation one declines."

There was a softness to her consonants, a hint of French not from Paris but from porches and parishes.

"If this is about business," Camille said, "my assistant handles my calendar during office hours. You can—"

"Oh, this is about business," the woman said. "And pleasure. And debt. Not necessarily in that order."

The hairs along Camille's arms prickled. She moved to the window without quite deciding to, watching the rain streak the glass, turn the street into a glossy black ribbon.

"If this is some kind of sales pitch," she said, "I am *not*—"

"You met me in the parking garage."

The words dropped into the space between them like a stone into deep water.

For a heartbeat, Camille heard the echo of fluorescent lights and the distant thud of car doors, smelled concrete and ozone. The woman by the pillar, in the black dress and red scarf, the tarnished scales at her hip.

"You didn't introduce yourself," Camille said.

"We're correcting that now." The voice warmed, just a little. "My name is Mireille. I thought it polite to tell you I'll be at Belle Rive. I would hate for you to be...surprised."

Camille's gaze slid to the envelope on the counter, to the small cursive addition near the bottom of the list. Someone had taken a pen and inserted Mireille's name so neatly it might have been printed there all along.

"How do you know I haven't already decided to decline?"

On the line, Mireille laughed softly, like a match flaring. "Because you, Ms. Durant, do not walk away from a room full of people who owe you, or think you might someday owe them. Especially not when the room is a house that has held every ugly thing this state has ever done and never once confessed."

The words settled over Camille's shoulders like a shawl: heavy, uninvited, exactly her size.

"And what do you think Belle Rive wants from me?" she asked.

"Not Belle Rive," Mireille said. "Houses don't want. They remember. They whisper. They observe. But houses don't want. It's the people who want. LeBlanc wants to make a problem go away. The others want money, power, absolution, revenge. And you—"

"I haven't said I want anything."

"Lie to them if you like," Mireille said. "You don't have to lie to me. You **can't** lie to me. Not really anyway. And you certainly can't lie to yourself."

Camille turned away from the window. On the screen, a mother clutched a framed photograph, her mouth moving around words the caption reduced to one line: "We didn't get justice. Our family was denied the justice we were promised. The system has failed us."

"Why are you calling me?" Camille asked.

"Consider it professional courtesy," Mireille said. "We are both in the business of outcomes, Miss Durant. Belle Rive will ask something of you. So will I. I thought you'd appreciate fair notice."

"Is that what you call it?"

"What would you call it?"

Camille thought of the way the jury foreman's hand had shaken when he read the words "not guilty." The way Kline's eyes had littered, bright and mean, when the cameras turned his way. The way her own hand had not shaken at all—until afterward, alone, when she'd reached for her keys and dropped them.

She looked at the invitation again, at the shiny silvery ink, the neat promise of a weekend that would be written up later as "strategic retreat" or "philanthropic summit."

"I suppose, advance disclosure," she said. "Theoretically."

Mireille chuckled. "Spoken like a lawyer."

The rain beat harder against the glass.

"I'm not promising I'll go," Camille said.

"Of course not. You will decide. That's what you're good at." A pause. "Do bring something nice to wear. Some occasions deserve respect."

"What kind of occasion?"

"The kind," Mireille said, "where someone will die, and everyone will insist they are shocked."

The line clicked. She was gone.

Camille stood there for a long moment, phone in hand. Then she set the phone down next to the envelope and turned the television off mid-sentence. The room dropped into a hush that was not quite silence.

On the counter, the invitation lay like a dark verdict waiting to be read. Camille picked it up one more time, ran her thumb along the edge, and then, with a small, controlled sigh, set it apart from the rest of the mail—a separate stack, a separate problem.

"I haven't said yes," she told the empty room. The empty room, sensibly, did not argue.

Outside, the storm settled in, as if it had all the time in the world.

Chapter 2
Residuals

By morning, the city had already decided what the Kline verdict meant.

"Justice system under fire," one talk radio host barked between ads for truck dealerships and injury lawyers. "Money buys freedom, that's the headline." On another station, a softer voice called it "a sober reminder that the burden of proof protects us all." They said "burden of proof" like a prayer or a curse, depending which side they'd wanted to win.

Camille let them talk while she drove, the radio turned low enough that the words blurred into a hum of outrage and rationalization. She knew all the arguments by heart. She'd made half of them herself, over years and cases she barely remembered.

Traffic crawled along the river, brake lights blooming red against the dull silver of the water. Humidity pressed at the windshield, sticky even with the air conditioning on. Her temples pulsed with the beginnings of a headache she refused to name.

At the third red light, a caller's voice cut through the static. "He killed my cousin," the man said, voice shaking. "You

understand? He killed my cousin. And that lawyer—Durant?—
she smiles like it's a game."

Camille's hand tightened on the steering wheel. She didn't
remember smiling. She remembered keeping her face as still as
stone while Kline's wife sobbed into his shoulder and the
victims' families stared at her like she'd personally cut their
throats.

She flicked the radio off and let silence pour into the car.

On her passenger seat, a file folder slid with the movement of
the car. KLINE, R. – PEOPLE V. KLINE, the tab read in her own
careful handwriting. She reached over, touched the cardboard
with two fingers, then pulled her hand back.

"Done," she said out loud. "We're done."

It didn't feel done.

By the time she reached the courthouse, the rain had settled into
a sullen drizzle. The building loomed out of the gray, concrete
stained darker in streaks where water had tracked the same
paths for years. She flashed her ID at security, let the metal
detector beep uselessly at her earrings, and took the familiar
climb up the stone steps.

Work is simple, she told herself. *Work has rules.*

The hallway outside her office still smelled faintly of old coffee
and floor polish. Her name—C. DURANT—was etched on the

14

frosted glass in neat black letters. She unlocked the door, stepped into the cool, dim space, and flicked on the lamp rather than the overhead fluorescents.

The Kline file went onto the credenza with a dull slap. She set her briefcase beside it, hung her blazer over the back of her chair, and took a slow breath.

Her inbox pulsed with new emails. Messages from her firm's senior partners, from reporters, from colleagues wanting the inside scoop. A subject line from one of the partners read: EXCELLENT WORK ON KLINE—FOLLOW-UP OPP.

She clicked that one open first.

> *Camille,*
> *The board is very pleased with yesterday's outcome. Kline's people have hinted at "expanding the relationship" and there may be other clients in his network in need of our services. Let's discuss next steps re: media strategy and potential future representation.*
>
> *Lunch?*
> *— R.*

She stared at the word "pleased" until it blurred, then typed a two-line reply and sent it before she could talk herself into writing what she was actually thinking.

Her phone buzzed on the desk. She swiped away a mindfulness app reminder and instead opened her browser. DARRYL JAMES, she typed into the search bar.

The results popped up instantly. She'd read these articles before.

BELOVED COMMUNITY LEADER CLEARED OF DUI CHARGES.

LOCAL BUSINESSMAN ACQUITTED IN FATAL CRASH SUES CITY FOR DEFAMATION.

NEW ALLEGATIONS EMERGE AGAINST JAMES INDUSTRIES.

She scrolled past the oldest pieces and found the newer ones.

INVESTIGATION LINKS JAMES INDUSTRIES TO DEADLY CHEMICAL LEAK.

FAMILIES SUE OVER TOXIC SPILL; CLAIM COMPANY IGNORED WARNINGS.

Among the thumbnails, a photo: a cluster of people holding candles near a chain-link fence, faces lit from below. In the center, a woman in a Saints hoodie held a picture of a boy. The caption beneath: "He was going to be the first in our family to go to college."

Camille clicked the article and forced herself to read it all the way through.

The leak had happened two years after she'd walked Darryl James out of a courtroom with no jail time and a suspended license he'd circumvented with a driver and brazen disregard for anyone's safety. Two years after she'd stood beside him for the cameras while he murmured about "healing" and "second chances."

The article detailed dates, times, warnings ignored, corners cut. Nowhere did it mention Camille Durant. The law didn't see a straight line from her cross-examination to the corroded pipe that finally burst.

But she saw the line. Thin and bright and unbroken.

"Stop," she muttered, closing the tab. "Stop it."

She sat back, rubbed her eyes with the heels of her hands. Behind the darkness, an image surfaced: a woman in a black dress with a red scarf and eyes like polished stone.

This is not the kind of invitation one declines.

She opened the top drawer of her desk and pulled out her wallet. Tucked behind her bar card was a business card she didn't remember putting there—black stock, nothing but a symbol embossed in silver: scales, tilted slightly off-balance.

Belle Rive.

Her email pinged again. This time, a message from someone she hadn't expected: Rafael Navarro, assistant DA, eternal thorn in her side, and one of the few people who could walk into her office without needing an appointment.

She had just finished reading his opening line—*You busy?*—when the man himself appeared in her doorway without knocking.

"Durant," he said. "Tell me you're not reading your own press."

Camille looked up to see Rafael leaning in the doorframe, file under one arm, tie already loosened. He had a talent for materializing exactly when you didn't want him to.

"I try not to," she said. "I prefer to let you do it for me. Keeps you angry. Sharpened." She winked deviously.

He smirked, stepped inside, and dropped into the chair opposite her desk without waiting to be asked. "Trust me, I'm sharp enough. Nice work yesterday. If you consider letting a double killer walk 'nice.'"

He said it lightly, but his eyes were searching her face.

"Jury did their job," she said. "I did mine."

"Depends how you feel about ghosts."

He slid the file onto her desk. No label on the tab yet. Just a thin rubber band holding it together.

She raised an eyebrow but didn't reach for it. "If this is about Kline—"

"It's not." He hesitated, which she did not like. Navarro rarely hesitated. "You remember that old James case you handled? The DUI with the kids?"

Her mouth went dry. "I remember."

"Figured." He nodded at the file. "Someone upstairs is putting together a task force. Environmental, corporate negligence, all that fun. James Industries is on the board. Apparently, between the leak and a few...other incidents, the feds are sniffing around."

"Other incidents?" she asked, even though she knew she didn't want the answer.

"Two former employees dead in the last year. Officially accidents." He shrugged one shoulder. "Unofficially, no one believes in that much bad luck."

The word *luck* scraped along her nerves.

"What does this have to do with me?" she asked.

"Technically? Nothing." He spread his hands. "You're clean. You did your job, they did theirs. But somebody in the AG's office thought you might have...insight. Into how your client operated. His patterns."

He sat back, his gaze still on her. "You're in his orbit, Durant. Doesn't matter whether you want to be or not."

Her fingers found the edge of the file and pressed, leaving little half-moons in the cardboard.

"I'm not in his orbit," she said quietly. "I defended him. That's over."

"If you say so." Navarro stood, smoothing his tie down more from habit than effect. "Take a look. Or don't. They'll build a case with or without you. But if you know something that could stop more bodies dropping, maybe this is your chance to balance the scales a little."

His eyes flicked to the black card on her desk, to the tiny silver scales, then back to her face.

"Close the door on your way out," she said.

He did, leaving the office smaller and darker without him.

For a long minute, Camille sat perfectly still. The rain tapped at the narrow high window like impatient fingers.

Then she pulled the James file closer. Opened it. Stared at the first page without really reading. Names, dates, phrases like "alleged pattern of negligence" and "possible homicide disguised as accident."

> *Someone will die, and everyone will insist they are shocked.*

Mireille's voice curled through her memory, soft and certain.

Camille closed the file and reached for the Belle Rive invitation in her bag. She laid it on top of the James folder and the little black card, making a neat, damning stack.

She picked up her pen and, before she could think better of it, on a small pad on her desk, she wrote the date from the Belle Rive card. In small, precise letters just below it, she wrote:

Find out what they want.

The ink sank into the paper, dark and permanent.

Outside, the rain continued its patient work, washing the city clean of nothing at all.

Chapter 2.5
First Miracle

Camille Durant was three years out of law school, green enough that optimism still edged out cynicism, when she took the case no one else would touch. *State v. Hollis*. Mid-level hustler accused of assaulting two women outside a Magazine Street bar—battered faces, clear eyewitnesses, his prints on the broken bottle. Slam dunk for the DA. Her boss called it a "loser's special"—good for billing hours, bad for résumés.

"Pass," she'd told him. "I'm not here to pad stats."

He'd laughed. "Everyone deserves representation, Durant. Even the guilty ones."

She took it anyway. Not for principle. For the courtroom practice. For the chance to cross-examine without a senior partner breathing down her neck. Hollis was oily-charming in intake, swearing the women came at him first, self-defense all the way. She half-believed him. Enough to build a story around it.

Prep was standard: witness lists, police reports, Hollis's spotty priors. The chain-of-custody form for the bottle arrived late, stamped "evidence locker." Camille filed it without a second glance—crossed her t's, dotted the prosecution's i's.

Trial day dawned muggy, the kind of heat that stuck clothes to skin. Courthouse smelled of stale coffee and desperation. Camille in her one good suit, nerves humming. DA was a veteran named Hargrove, paunchy and smug, the type who collected wins like baseball cards.

Jury selection went fine—six women, balanced demographics, no one glaring outright. Opening statements: Hargrove painted Hollis as predator. Camille countered with "incomplete story," "rival accounts," "rush to judgment." Solid, if unremarkable.

Prosecution's case opened strong: victim one on the stand, voice cracking, bruises still yellowing. Victim two nodding along. Eyewitness swearing to the bottle swing. Then the bottle itself— bagged, tagged, ready for the custodian.

"Chain of custody?" Hargrove prompted.

Custodian shuffled forward, balding clerk with wire-rimmed glasses. Camille had seen her before—Émiline something, quiet type who handled records. She flipped open her logbook, frowned. "Uh... form's missing, sir."

Hargrove blinked. "Missing?"

"Logged intake," Émiline said, voice even, eyes flicking past Camille without pause. "But the transfer sheet from evidence to here... can't locate it." She tapped the empty page. "Must've been misfiled."

24

Hargrove blustered. "Misfiled? This is a murder weapon—"

"Assault," Camille corrected mildly. "And without the chain, Your Honor?"

Judge Landry peered over his glasses. "Objection sustained. Bottle excluded."

Hargrove's case wobbled. Eyewitness crumbled on cross—drunk, bad angle, "maybe" it was Hollis. Victims' timelines frayed under polite questions about the bar fight's lead-up. By close, the DA was reduced to passion pleas.

Jury out four hours. Camille waited in the hall, stomach knotted, Hollis pacing like a caged animal. "Told you," he grinned. "Self-defense."

Verdict: not guilty.

Camille exhaled, hand not shaking until she hit the restroom mirror. Twenty-eight, undefeated in solo trials. Her phone buzzed—boss: *Nice work. Drinks?*

She texted back, *"Rain check,"* and splashed water on her face. The high buzzed electric, better than coffee or courtroom wins. *Everyone deserves representation.* She'd believed it then.

Down in records pickup, grabbing her copies, Émiline was at the desk—filing something innocuous. Their eyes met. The clerk paused, scales pendant at her neck glinting odd, unbalanced.

"Some cases want to be won," she said softly. "You were there to catch it."

Camille nodded, buzz fading to unease. "Luck of the draw."

Émiline smiled, thin. "Draws have hands."

Camille left without asking. Outside, rain slicked the steps. She drove home windows down, adrenaline singing. First miracle. Wouldn't be the last.

In her kitchen, bills piled high, she poured a bourbon neat. Toasted the mirror: *You're good at this.* The taste burned clean, and she slept like stone.

Chapter 3
Belle Rive & The LeBlancs

The public library's research section wasn't pretty. Neither was the internet café on Toulouse, where Camille rented an hour of privacy and a pot of coffee that tasted like aluminum. She spent two days gathering what was available without raising questions: deeds and property transfers, society pages, a feature in *Louisiana Homes* from 2003 about Belle Rive's restoration.

Belle Rive had been built in 1847. The LeBlancs had owned it since 1889—the postwar generation seizing opportunity the way their ancestors seized land. The 2003 article called it "a jewel of antebellum architecture, carefully restored to honor Louisiana's complex legacy." The photographs showed white columns, a wraparound porch, gardens that had been tended back into submission, a ballroom with a crystal chandelier that cost more than most houses.

The current matriarch was Adeline LeBlanc, seventy-eight, widow of the late developer and speculator Claude LeBlanc who'd made his fortune in commercial real estate and land deals. Adeline had been a socialite, a patron of the arts, and—according to one carefully worded profile—"a woman who understood how power worked in Louisiana."

There were children: a son, Étienne, who worked in finance in

New York but returned frequently; a daughter, Delphine, who ran a PR firm in Baton Rouge and handled the family's public image. A younger son from Claude's first marriage, Antoine, who'd made a career in politics and was rumored to be eyeing a congressional seat.

The LeBlancs hosted events for the city's movers. Charity galas. Political fundraisers. Strategy sessions that were never written about but were known, in the way that important things are, to happen behind those white columns.

On her third morning of research, Camille found something useful: a lawsuit filed in 1998, *State v. Claude LeBlanc*, alleging kickbacks on a municipal development project. The charges had been quietly dropped after a months-long investigation. The local paper had run a small piece on the dismissal—"LEBLANC SUIT DISMISSED ON PROCEDURAL GROUNDS"—with no explanation of what procedural grounds.

Camille knew what that meant. A key witness had suddenly become unavailable. A document trail had gone cold. The prosecutor handling it—a man named Robert Dufrane—had moved to federal court two months later. A lucrative position with a private firm had materialized shortly after.

She closed the browser without saving anything. Some knowledge was dangerous to retain in searchable form.

That evening, she called the number on the Belle Rive invitation.

28

A woman answered on the second ring. Efficient, older, with a Creole accent that softened her words.

"LeBlanc residence. How may I help you?"

"This is Camille Durant. I'd like to confirm my attendance for the weekend of the fourteenth."

A pause. The sound of pages turning.

"Of course, Ms. Durant. We are delighted. Arrival Friday at four o'clock, departure Sunday afternoon. Transportation from the airport can be arranged if needed."

"I'll drive myself," Camille said. "What's the dress code?"

"Casual elegant for Friday evening, formal for Saturday dinner. Sunday is informal—guests depart by noon."

Everything very organized. Very controlled.

"One question," Camille said. "The invitation mentions 'matters of mutual interest.' Can you tell me anything about what Madame LeBlanc intends to discuss?"

Another pause, longer.

"Madame LeBlanc prefers to address such matters in person, Ms. Durant. You understand, I'm sure—discretion."

"Of course," Camille said. "I'll see her on the fourteenth."

She hung up and sat for a long time in the darkness of her office.

Outside, the river moved black and silent.

Belle Rive was two hours north, past the swamplands, where the ground was older and less forgiving. The house waited in that landscape like a secret someone had forgotten how to keep.

Camille pulled up her calendar and, without quite believing she was doing it, marked the date. Underlined it. Wrote, in small letters in the margin: *Point of no return.*

Three days before she was due to leave, her mother called.

"Camille, darling. I saw the news about your case. The Kline gentleman." Her mother's voice had the carefully maintained quality of old money and older manners. "Everyone's talking about it."

"I'm sure they are," Camille said, cradling the phone against her shoulder while she packed her laptop.

"Mrs. Guidry said it was a travesty. But I told her, I said, 'My daughter believes in the law. She believes everyone deserves representation.'"

"Thank you, Maman."

"You do believe that, don't you?"

The question hung in the air between them, weighted with something Camille couldn't quite name.

"Yes," she said. "I do."

"Good." A pause. "Your father would be proud."

Camille's hand stilled on the zipper of her bag. Her father, who'd died with his reputation intact and his conscience buried so deep no one would ever excavate it.

"I have to go, Maman. I have a work thing this weekend."

"Of course. You're always so busy. Call me when you're back?"

"I will."

She hung up and stood in the middle of her living room, surrounded by the trappings of a life she'd built on the promise that competence was enough, that skill could substitute for certainty.

On her kitchen counter, the Belle Rive invitation gleamed like a dare.

Camille picked up her overnight bag, checked that she had the black card with the silver scales, and walked out into the Louisiana night without looking back.

Chapter 4
Arrival

The rain had been threatening all day, a weight in the air like a held breath. By the time Camille turned off the main highway, the sky had darkened to the color of old brass, and the first real drops were beginning to strike the windshield in heavy, deliberate patterns.

She drove slowly. The landscape had changed—less city, less clear definition of where one property ended and another began. Trees crowded the road, Spanish moss hanging from their branches like hair that needed washing. A glimpse of swamp to her left: black water, cypress knees jutting up like fingers.

The road to Belle Rive wound through a small forest, oak-lined and narrow. When she emerged, the house was there suddenly, as though the trees had been holding it out of sight until the last moment.

It was both more and less impressive than the photographs. Larger, in person. The columns had a stained, weary quality no feature article could convey. The grounds were beautiful in a high-maintenance way—the grass manicured, the flowers arranged too carefully, the whole effect suggesting that nature was being held at gunpoint, forced to behave.

Camille parked behind a Mercedes sedan and a Range Rover.

Three other cars were already there—a Porsche, a Lincoln, a sleek BMW. People with money. People with places to be and no patience for traffic.

The rain intensified as she climbed the porch steps, her small overnight bag clutched against her side. Before she could knock, the door swung open.

"Ms. Durant!" A woman with iron-gray hair pulled into an elegant chignon, wearing a crisp white blouse and pearls. "Welcome to Belle Rive. I'm Céleste, Madame LeBlanc's daughter. Please, come in before the sky falls."

The foyer was exactly what Camille expected: high ceiling, chandelier that gleamed like ice, the sense of a space designed to make you feel small. There was a smell—furniture polish, magnolia, something older underneath, like soil and river water.

"The others have assembled in the drawing room," Céleste said, gesturing to a doorway off the main hall. "Dinner will be at seven. Would you like me to show you to your room first? You're in the east wing, lovely views of the grounds."

"Yes, please," Camille said.

The east wing smelled like fresh linen and old money. Her room was decorated in shades of cream and gold, with a four-poster bed and windows overlooking gardens that sloped toward darker trees. There was a marble bathroom with an absurd number of towels and a framed needlepoint—"Bless This House and All Who Enter"—hanging above the vanity like a warning disguised as blessing.

Camille changed into an ivory silk blouse and tailored charcoal slacks—casual elegant, as requested—checked her phone for messages from her office (three, all manageable), and turned it on silent. Then she steeled herself and went downstairs.

The drawing room opened onto a receiving hall where roughly a dozen people were already assembled, drinks in hand. Camille recognized some faces from news photos, from courtroom encounters, from the careful research she'd done. She placed them mentally: State Senator Gerard Mouton, red-faced and jovial; a property developer named Vincent Thibodeaux, nervous energy radiating from him like heat; a woman she vaguely remembered from a charity ball years ago, introduced now as Patricia Arceneaux, "family friend and legal counsel."

At the center of the room sat a woman in her late seventies, silver-haired and regal, wearing a dove-gray dress that probably cost more than Camille's car. Adeline LeBlanc. She held court from a high-backed chair upholstered in burgundy velvet, and everyone around her was listening the way people listen when someone has demonstrated they can hurt them.

A younger man stood near the French doors, fingers wrapped around a glass of bourbon, watching the gathering with the detached attention of someone performing a social obligation. That would be Étienne, the son from New York. A woman in her forties worked the room with practiced ease, making introductions, refreshing drinks—Delphine, the PR daughter.

And near the window, dressed in deep purple silk with her hair pulled back in an elaborate twist, was a woman with dark eyes and a smile that registered as pure calculation.

Mireille.

She inclined her head slightly when Camille's eyes found her, an acknowledgment of the contract between them: *We know the real reason we're here.*

"Ah!" Adeline LeBlanc's voice cut through the murmur of conversation. Her accent was cultured Creole, each word precisely placed. "The formidable Ms. Durant. Come, child, you must meet everyone."

What followed was a ritual as choreographed as any court proceeding: handshakes, pleasantries, the careful evaluation of each other. The senator was jovial and drank too much. The property developer was nervous, his eyes flickering between Adeline and a woman Camille guessed was his wife. Patricia Arceneaux was sharp-eyed and assessing. Étienne barely acknowledged her presence beyond a curt nod.

"We're so pleased you could make it," Patricia said, her smile tight. "Adeline speaks so highly of your work."

"That's kind of her," Camille said. "Though I suspect Madame LeBlanc and I have only had professional contact."

"Professional contact is often the most meaningful," Adeline said from her chair, not rising. "It reveals character in ways social niceties never can. You defended Claude's business associate some years ago. Mr. Thibodeaux's partner, I believe? A zoning matter?"

Camille remembered. A developer accused of bribing city officials. She'd gotten the charges reduced to a fine.

"I remember," Camille said carefully.

"You were very effective." Adeline's smile didn't reach her eyes. "As you've been in so many cases since."

The room had gone quiet in that way rooms do when everyone is pretending not to listen while hanging on every word.

"I do my job," Camille said.

"Yes," Adeline said. "You certainly do."

Dinner was served promptly at seven in a dining room that could have seated twenty and felt intimate with twelve. The table was set with china so fine it was nearly translucent, and the conversation moved with the precision of a legal argument: a statement, a counterpoint, a new direction, always careful, always measured.

But underneath the pleasantries, tension moved like a current. No one wanted to be here. Or rather: everyone wanted to *be* here but no one wanted to be *seen* here. The atmosphere had the strained quality of people pretending they hadn't made deals in dark offices, hadn't received envelopes, hadn't learned to look away from certain kinds of suffering.

Adeline held court from the head of the table, telling a story about a development project in New Orleans—"the city's greatest opportunity for reinvestment," she called it, though what she meant was displacement and profit. The others laughed at the appropriate moments. No one challenged her.

Camille found herself seated between Patricia and a man who'd been introduced as Father Dominic Rousseau, a priest who served on several nonprofit boards the LeBlancs supported. He blessed the meal in Latin and then spent the first course explaining, unprompted, why the Church's position on certain social matters was "more nuanced than the media portrayed."

Across the table, Mireille caught her eye and raised her wine glass a fraction of an inch. A silent toast: *Welcome to hell. Mind the complimentary breadbaskets.*

Toward the end of the meal, when the wine had loosened tongues just enough, Senator Mouton leaned forward with calculated casualness.

"I have to ask, Adeline," he said. "Why the lawyers? Present company excluded," he nodded at Camille and Patricia, "but you've got three defense attorneys here and a woman who advises on settlement negotiations. Are we expecting trouble?"

The table stilled.

Adeline smiled, untroubled. "On the contrary, Senator. I find that having the right people in the room prevents trouble. Ms. Durant comes highly recommended as someone who understands the...complexities of difficult situations. And Mireille—" she turned to her with a smile that was just fractionally too warm, "—Mireille understands the importance of balance."

Mireille met her gaze without expression. "I understand that everything has a price," she said. "And that debts come due."

"Exactly," Adeline said. "Which is why I wanted everyone here together. To discuss how we move forward. How we ensure that—" she paused, choosing her words carefully, "—that past obligations don't become future complications."

The rain had intensified outside. Camille could hear it against the windows, a sound like something trying to get in.

"What kind of obligations?" asked a younger woman Camille hadn't been introduced to—one of the granddaughters, perhaps, or a family friend. Her voice was careful, almost delicate, but her hands gripped the edge of the table.

"Nothing dire," Adeline said smoothly. "Just some old business that's been resolved in ways that certain people might find inconvenient to remember. I want to ensure we're all on the same page about how we handle inquiries. Should any arise."

Camille felt the room shift. This was it. This was why she was here. Not to defend anyone—not yet. But to be seen as someone who could be trusted to make problems disappear. To make inconvenient truths invisible.

Across the table, Mireille caught her eye again, and this time there was no humor in her expression. Only a kind of solemn recognition: *This is the moment. This is the choice.*

Before Camille could respond, before anyone could respond, the sound of tires on gravel echoed from outside, followed by a car door slamming.

Delphine rose quickly. "That's odd. We're not expecting anyone else."

A moment later, footsteps on the porch, urgent and heavy. Then a knock—not the polite tap of a guest, but the sharp rap of authority.

Céleste moved to answer it, but Adeline raised one hand. "Let Antoine get it. He's expecting a courier."

But Antoine, the younger son, hadn't moved from his place at the far end of the table. He looked as confused as everyone else.

The knock came again, more insistent.

Finally, Céleste went to the foyer. They heard the door open, heard voices—Céleste's measured tones and a man's voice, urgent and official.

When Céleste returned, her face was carefully blank, but there was something in her eyes that made Camille's stomach tighten.

"Madame," Céleste said quietly. "There's a Detective Broussard here. He says there's been a death. He's asking if anyone here knows a Mr. Marcus Kline."

The room went absolutely silent.

Camille's wine glass stopped halfway to her lips. She set it down carefully, aware that everyone was about to turn and look at her.

"Kline?" Senator Mouton said. "The businessman? I thought he was just acquitted—"

"He was," Camille said, her voice steadier than she felt.

"Three days ago."

Adeline's gaze fixed on her, sharp and assessing. "Ms. Durant. I believe Mr. Kline was your client?"

"He was."

"Well then," Adeline said, rising from her chair with the deliberate grace of someone who'd spent a lifetime controlling rooms. "Perhaps you should speak with the detective. The rest of us will adjourn to the library."

It wasn't a suggestion.

Camille stood, feeling the weight of every eye in the room. As she moved toward the foyer, Mireille's voice drifted after her, pitched just loud enough to carry:

"How interesting. Someone will die, and everyone will insist they are shocked."

Chapter 5
Old Case, New Wounds

Detective Luc Broussard was exactly what Camille expected: mid-forties, weathered face, cheap suit slightly damp from the rain, and eyes that had seen enough bullshit to recognize it from across a parish. He stood in the foyer with his hat in his hands, water dripping onto Adeline LeBlanc's immaculate marble floor.

"Ms. Durant?" he said when Camille approached. "Detective Broussard, St. Tammany Parish. Sorry to interrupt your evening."

"What happened to Marcus Kline?" Camille asked.

"That's what we're trying to figure out." He pulled a small notebook from his jacket. "He was found dead in his home this afternoon. Housekeeper called it in around three PM. We're treating it as suspicious."

"Suspicious how?"

"Can't say much at this stage. But given his recent acquittal and the, ah, public attention on that case, we're being thorough. His attorney of record was listed as you, so I wanted to notify you directly. Professional courtesy."

Camille's mind raced. "How did he die?"

"Coroner's preliminary says heart attack. But there are some inconsistencies at the scene. Things that don't quite add up." He glanced past her to where the dinner party guests were slowly filtering into the library, casting curious glances their way. "You're here with quite a group."

"Family gathering," Camille said smoothly. "I'm a guest of Madame LeBlanc."

"Hm." He made a note. "When's the last time you spoke with Mr. Kline?"

"The day of the verdict. I called to advise him on media requests. He thanked me for my work. That was it."

"He seem worried about anything? Threats? Anyone who might want to hurt him?"

> *Only the families of the people he killed,* Camille thought. *And anyone with a conscience.*

"He mentioned that he'd received some angry calls and messages," she said. "But nothing specific. Nothing that rose to the level of an actionable threat."

"Right." More notes. "You'll be available for follow-up questions? We may need a formal statement."

"Of course. I'll be here through Sunday, then back in the city."

"Good enough." He tucked the notebook away. "Sorry again for the interruption. Enjoy your weekend."

He said it like he knew that was now impossible.

Camille watched him walk back out into the rain, saw his taillights disappear down the oak-lined drive. Then she stood alone in the foyer for a long moment, listening to the murmur of conversation from the library, the sound of the storm intensifying outside.

Marcus Kline was dead.

Three days after she'd gotten him acquitted.

The timing felt wrong. Everything felt wrong.

She found Mireille in the library, standing by the window with a glass of red wine, watching the storm.

"You knew," Camille said quietly, coming to stand beside her.

"I knew someone would die," Mireille said. "I didn't know who. Or when. Only that it was inevitable."

"Because of the magic? The current?"

"Because of the imbalance." Mireille turned to look at her. "You tilted the scales, chère. You pulled strings—knowingly or not—to keep a guilty man from facing justice. The universe doesn't like that. It corrects."

"He had a heart attack. That's not—" Camille stopped. "The detective said there were inconsistencies."

"There always are," Mireille said. "When the current takes what it's owed, it leaves signs. Little wrongnesses. Things that don't quite make sense to people who only see the material world."

Camille's hands were shaking. She clasped them together. "You're saying the current killed him?"

"I'm saying the debt was called. How it was collected..." Mireille shrugged. "That depends on many things. Who did the working. What they offered in exchange. How precise their intent was."

"Who did the working?" Camille asked. "You?"

"No." Mireille's gaze was steady. "I don't work for acquittals, chère. I work for balance. Whoever helped you—whoever tipped those scales in your favor—they're the one who set this in motion."

"I didn't ask anyone to—"

"Didn't you?" Mireille's voice was soft but cutting. "Every time you took a case you knew was hopeless, every time evidence mysteriously disappeared or witnesses changed their stories, every time you chalked it up to 'luck'—you were asking. You just didn't know what language you were speaking."

Across the library, Adeline was holding court with Senator Mouton and Patricia, their voices low and urgent. Étienne had

46

disappeared—probably to his room or to make phone calls. Delphine was managing the younger guests, keeping the atmosphere from dissolving into panic.

Father Rousseau approached, his face arranged in practiced sympathy. "Ms. Durant. I heard about your client. I'm so sorry. If you need to talk, or if you'd like to pray—"

"I'm fine, Father. Thank you."

He lingered, clearly wanting to say more, but Camille turned back to the window, and eventually he drifted away.

"The host knew this would happen," Camille said quietly. "Adeline. She invited us all here for a reason."

"She invited you here because she's terrified," Mireille said. "She's old, and powerful, and she's made a great many deals over the years. Some of them with me. Some of them with others. And now she feels the current shifting. She wants to make sure when it comes for what it's owed, she's not the one who pays."

"That's why the lawyers. She wants legal protection."

"Legal and otherwise." Mireille swirled her wine. "She thinks if she gathers enough clever people in one place, one of them will find a loophole. A way to cheat the bill."

"Can she?"

"What do you think?"

Camille thought of the courtroom, of the judge's gavel, of Marcus Kline walking free into the sunlight. Of the families watching from the gallery, their faces twisted with grief and rage.

She thought of Darryl James and his chemical leak.

She thought of every case she'd won that she shouldn't have.

"No," she said. "I don't think she can."

"Then you're smarter than she is," Mireille said. "The question now is: what are you going to do about it?"

Before Camille could answer, Delphine appeared at her elbow, all professional concern. "Ms. Durant, I'm so sorry about your client. If you need anything—a phone, privacy, a car to take you back to the city—please just say the word."

"I'm staying," Camille said. The words surprised her, but as soon as she said them, she knew they were true. "Thank you, though."

Delphine nodded and moved on to manage the next small crisis.

The dinner party had fractured. Half the guests had retreated upstairs. The others lingered in tight clusters, speaking in hushed tones. The storm battered the windows, and somewhere in the house, a door slammed.

48

Camille found a chair in a corner and sat, her mind racing through possibilities. Heart attack. Suspicious circumstances. The detective's careful phrasing. *Things that don't quite add up.*

She pulled out her phone and did a quick search:

MARCUS KLINE DEATH.

The news was already breaking.

LOCAL BUSINESSMAN FOUND DEAD DAYS AFTER CONTROVERSIAL ACQUITTAL.

She clicked through to a local news site. The article was sparse—body discovered by housekeeper, age fifty-three, apparent heart attack, investigation ongoing. Then, in the third paragraph:

> *Authorities noted unusual circumstances at the scene, including symbols drawn in what appeared to be ash near the body and the presence of burned legal documents in the fireplace. Police are investigating whether the death may be connected to recent threats Kline had received following his acquittal.*

Symbols. Burned legal documents.

Camille looked up to find Mireille watching her from across the room.

Their eyes met, and Mireille raised her glass in another silent toast.

Welcome to the game, chère. Let's see if you can figure out the rules before the next body drops.

Outside, thunder rolled across the bayou like a courthouse door slamming shut.

Chapter 5.5
Mireille, Watching

Mireille Baptiste sipped chicory from a chipped mug, perched on a stool in the courthouse basement break room. It was the kind of room nobody lingered in—vending machine humming stale, fridge rattling like it held grudges. Perfect for watching.

The current had tugged her here again. Another Durant verdict. Not the first, not the splashiest, but clean. Camille's client—a slick nonprofit darling, Marcus-type lite—walked on embezzlement charges that should've stuck. Witness recanted overnight. Accountant "found" conflicting ledgers mid-trial. Jury blinked, shrugged, acquitted.

Upstairs, Camille would be shaking hands, fielding backslaps. Down here, Mireille traced the scales on her mug. Émiline's work—subtle, surgical. A nudge here, a missing page there. Camille never saw the hand.

Door creaked. Émiline entered, arms full of files, pendant swinging unbalanced. "You again," she said, not surprised.

"Watching your protégé." Mireille set the mug down. "She's racking them up."

Émiline dumped files on the table. "System's broken. She tilts it right sometimes."

"Right for who?" Mireille's voice stayed soft. "Hollis girls still can't sleep. Today's mark stole from cancer kids."

Émiline's jaw tightened. "Intent matters. She fights clean."

Mireille leaned forward. "Clean wins rot. You know that."

Silence stretched. Émiline straightened a stack. "Claude pays well. Leverage for bigger balances."

Mireille stood. "She's hooked now. What happens when she questions the miracles?"

"She won't." Émiline met her eyes, steady. "Ambition blinds."

Mireille left without arguing. Up the stairs, past echoing halls. Camille's office light burned late. The current hummed content, scales tipping. For now.

But Mireille saw the tilt growing. One day it'd snap back.

Chapter 6

Night Conversations

The storm would not let them leave even if they wanted to.

By midnight, the rain had turned the long drive into a river of mud, and the weather service was calling it a tropical depression that had stalled over the parish. Belle Rive sat in its grip like a ship run aground, all its elegant guests trapped aboard.

Camille couldn't sleep. She'd tried—had lain in the four-poster bed staring at the ceiling while her mind turned over the facts like evidence at trial. Marcus Kline. Heart attack. Burned legal documents. Symbols in ash. Someone had staged his death to look like something more than natural causes. Or someone had actually made it something more than natural causes.

The distinction mattered.

At 1:15 a.m., she gave up, pulled a cardigan over her nightgown, and padded downstairs in bare feet. The house creaked and settled around her, the old wood adjusting to humidity and weight. Lightning flashed through the tall windows, throwing the furniture into sharp relief before plunging everything back into shadow.

She found the kitchen by following the smell of coffee. Someone else had the same idea.

Vincent Thibodeaux sat at the large farmhouse table, a mug between his hands, staring at nothing. The property developer who'd been so nervous at dinner now looked hollowed out, like someone had scooped the stuffing from him and left only the shell.

"Ms. Durant," he said when he saw her. "Couldn't sleep either?"

"No." She poured herself a cup from the pot on the counter, noted the bourbon bottle open beside it. "Mind if I join you?"

"Please." He gestured to the chair across from him. "Misery loves company, or so they say."

They sat in silence for a moment, listening to the rain hammer the roof.

"I knew him," Vincent said finally. "Kline. We worked together on a project five years ago. Commercial development out near Lake Pontchartrain. He was..." He trailed off, took a long swallow of his coffee. "He was a sonofabitch, if I'm being honest. Cut corners. Paid people off. But he didn't deserve to die like that."

"Like what?" Camille asked carefully.

"However he died. The detective made it sound like... I don't know. Like it wasn't clean." Vincent looked at her directly for the

54

first time. "You got him off three days ago. Now he's dead. That doesn't strike you as strange?"

"It strikes me as suspicious," Camille said. "Which is why the police are investigating."

"The police." Vincent laughed, a bitter sound. "The police investigate what they're told to investigate. You know that as well as I do. You know how this works—money changes hands, evidence disappears, people forget what they saw." He leaned forward. "That's why Adeline brought us here, isn't it? To make sure we all remember the right version of things?"

"What version is that?"

"The version where nobody looks too closely at who benefited from what. Where past... arrangements stay in the past." His hands were shaking around the mug. "I didn't want to come. My wife insisted. She said it would be rude to decline Madame LeBlanc's invitation. But I knew what this was. I knew—"

He stopped himself, seeming to realize he was saying too much to a woman who made her living weaponizing other people's admissions.

Camille set her coffee down. "Mr. Thibodeaux. Are you in some kind of trouble?"

"Aren't we all?" He stood abruptly, leaving his mug on the table.

"Get some sleep, Ms. Durant. Tomorrow's going to be a long day."

He left her alone in the kitchen with the storm and her thoughts.

"Enough," she told herself, and started back to her room.

On her way back upstairs, she heard voices from the conservatory—a haunting glass-walled room that jutted from the east side of the house, full of exotic plants that probably had complicated Latin names and required specialized care. The door was half-open. Camille stopped in the shadows of the hallway.

"—absolutely insane," a woman's voice was saying. Young, furious, barely controlled. "She's playing with people's lives."

"She's protecting the family." That was Antoine, Adeline's younger son, the politician. His voice had the practiced calm of someone used to managing volatile situations. "As she has always done."

"By inviting a dead man's lawyer? By bringing that—that witch into the house?"

"Mireille is a consultant."

"Mireille is a—" The woman bit off whatever she'd been about to say. "You know what she does, Antoine. You know what she is. And you're just going to let Mother drag us all into this?"

"What would you have me do, Isabelle?"

So that was who the young woman was—Isabelle LeBlanc, Antoine's daughter, early twenties, reportedly working for an environmental nonprofit. The idealistic one.

"Tell the truth," Isabelle said. "Walk away. Any of it would be better than sitting here waiting for—"

"For what?"

"For whatever happens next!" Her voice cracked. "Someone died, Antoine. And we're all sitting around pretending it's normal, pretending we don't know—"

"Lower your voice."

"Why? Afraid someone might hear? Afraid they'll figure out that this whole family is built on—"

The sound of a slap, sharp and sudden.

Silence.

Then Antoine's voice, very quiet: "You will not speak about this family that way. Do you understand?"

Camille didn't hear Isabelle's response. Footsteps approached the door, and she slipped quickly around the corner into an alcove, pressing herself against the wall. Antoine strode past, jaw set, hands clenched at his sides. A moment later, Isabelle followed, one hand pressed to her cheek, tears streaming silently down her face.

When they were gone, Camille let out a breath she didn't know she'd been holding.

Interesting. She wasn't sure what to think. when she was certain no one would see her, she continued back to her room.

She was halfway up the stairs when a voice spoke from the darkness of the landing above.

"You're wondering who did it."

Mireille materialized from the shadows like she'd been part of them. She wore a silk robe the color of blood, her hair loose around her shoulders, and somehow managed to look both perfectly awake and like she'd never needed sleep in the first place.

"I'm wondering a lot of things," Camille said.

"But mostly that." Mireille descended the stairs until they were eye-to-eye. "Who performed the working that killed Marcus Kline? Who has that kind of power? Who had access to your case files, to his personal effects, to the knowledge of what you'd done?"

"Do you know?"

"I have suspicions." Mireille touched the banister, and for a moment Camille could have sworn she saw something—a faint shimmer in the air, like heat rising from pavement. "The house is full of them. Secrets. Guilt. Unpaid debts. The current runs thick here, chère. Has for generations."

"The LeBlancs."

"Among others. This land remembers. Every oath ever sworn on it, every deal struck in these rooms, every corner cut and conscience buried." Mireille's eyes caught the lightning flash. "You feel it, don't you? That weight in the air. Like something's watching."

Camille did feel it. Had felt it since she arrived. "What does the house want?"

"As I said before, houses don't want. But the current does. It wants balance. It wants the books settled. And right now, Ms. Durant, your name is written in red ink on nearly every page."

"I didn't ask for magic to tip my cases."

"Didn't you?" Mireille stepped closer. "Every time you argued impossibly well, every time evidence vanished at just the right moment, every time a witness forgot what they saw—did you never wonder? Did you never feel the nudge, the little whisper in your ear saying this is your moment, take it?"

Camille wanted to say no. Wanted to say she'd won on skill alone.

But she remembered. She remembered the way the courtroom had felt during the James case, the moment the key witness had collapsed. She'd felt something then—a pull, a certainty, a sense that the world was arranging itself in her favor.

She'd called it luck.

"Someone's been helping you for years," Mireille said. "Someone with access to the current. Someone who wanted you to win, who needed you to win. And now that someone is collecting what they're owed."

"By killing my clients?"

"By correcting the imbalances. Three cases, I'd wager. The three worst ones, where justice was most thoroughly perverted. Darryl James, Marcus Kline, and one more." Mireille tilted her head. "Who's the third, chère? Which client keeps you up at night?"

Camille's mouth went dry.

She knew.

"Get some sleep," Mireille said, turning to go. "Tomorrow the second debt comes due, and you'll want to be sharp when it does. The house is watching, and it keeps very good records."

She vanished into the darkness, leaving Camille alone on the stairs with the sound of the storm and the weight of her own conscience.

Camille finally made it back to her room and stood at the window, watching lightning fracture the sky over the bayou.

Somewhere in the house, a door clicked shut.

Somewhere else, floorboards creaked.

And in the hallway outside her room, the lights flickered—once, twice, three times—before settling back to their normal glow.

She thought about Vincent Thibodeaux's fear, about Isabelle's fury, about the slap and the tears and the weight of secrets this family carried.

She thought about Mireille's question: Who's the third?

And she thought about the file Rafael had brought her, the one she hadn't opened fully, the one with Darryl James's name on the tab and a list of bodies in the margins.

Three cases.

She pulled out her phone and opened her secure files, scrolling through case numbers until she found what she was looking for.

State v. Margot Devereux.

The gallery owner. The art fraud case. Camille had gotten her off on a technicality—an illegal search that tainted the entire evidence chain. Margot had walked out of that courtroom and six months later had been connected to a forgery ring that defrauded collectors out of millions. One of them, an elderly man who'd invested his life savings, had died of a stress-induced heart attack when he learned the truth.

Three cases where her victories had enabled further, far greater harm.

Three debts to be paid.

Thunder rolled, closer this time.

Camille put the phone away and climbed into bed, knowing she wouldn't sleep, knowing that tomorrow would bring more news she didn't want to hear.

Outside her window, the oak trees bent and twisted in the wind, their branches scraping against the glass like fingers trying to get in.

And somewhere in the house, someone else was awake, watching, waiting for the scales to balance themselves one death at a time.

Chapter 6.5

Another Miracle

Belle Rive's guest room pressed close, silk sheets twisted around Camille's legs like accusations. Sleep wouldn't come. The coffee soured in her gut, Kline's death replaying, Mireille's voice curling through the dark:

Whoever helped you tipped those scales. They set this in motion.

The memory pulled her under, sharp as a witness recall.

Five years back. *State v. Ellis.* The defendant was a nonprofit darling—golden boy with glossy brochures and tearful testimonials, accused of fleecing widows and orphans through shell charities. Ledgers didn't lie: transfers, falsified receipts, his signature bold on every page. Ironclad for the DA.

Camille had prepped without mercy. Motions to suppress shaky priors, character witnesses from his soup-kitchen days. Day three, the accountant took the stand—retired CPA, voice steady as he walked the jury through the numbers. Closing arguments tomorrow. Slam.

That night, Camille dreamed of tarnished scales, one pan sagging under black ink that bled like courtroom coffee.

Morning brought panic. Accountant's call at 7 a.m.: "Ms. Durant, the ledgers... conflicting copies surfaced overnight. My originals—they're gone from the evidence locker."

"Gone?" She'd gripped the phone, heart kicking.

"Custodian swears they logged them. Clerk's desk says misfiled. DA's furious."

Court convened. DA blustered. Judge Landry frowned at the chain-of-custody gap: dual versions, no clear provenance. "Your case wobbles without foundation, Counselor."

Camille pounced. "Reasonable doubt, Your Honor. If the state can't prove authenticity..."

Jury deliberated two hours. Verdict: not guilty.

Ellis crushed her in a hug outside, champagne flutes appearing from nowhere. "You're a miracle worker, Durant." Firm partners toasted her at dinner—backslaps, rounds on the house. The high thrummed electric, better than any prior win. This was why she'd gone to law school.

Weeks later, scrolling news over cold coffee, the rot surfaced. Ellis back in headlines—same scam, fresh widows ruined. One photo: empty ranch house foreclosed, pill bottle by an unmade bed. Suicide. Cancer fund victim.

Camille's stomach turned. Coincidence. Bad guy's gonna be bad. She'd closed the tab, poured more coffee.

Her partner clapped her shoulder next morning: "Heard about Ellis fallout. Tough break. But hell—another W on the board. Who's next?"

She'd smiled, throat tight. Took the case.

Now, sheets damp, Camille punched the pillow. Miracles soured. Every time. The current remembered. So did she.

Chapter 7
Breaking News of Second Death

Morning came pale and sick, the sky the color of old bruises. The storm hadn't moved on so much as it had sunk into the ground, leaving the lawns sodden and the drive converted into a churned mess of mud and standing water. Belle Rive felt like an isolated island.

Camille came downstairs to find most of the guests already assembled in the dining room, picking at breakfast with the enthusiasm of people being forced to wait for news they knew would be bad. The coffee was strong and the conversation weak—small talk delivered in voices that didn't even believe themselves.

Adeline presided from the head of the table in lavender silk, looking as fresh as if she'd slept a perfect eight hours, though Camille suspected she'd slept as poorly as the rest of them. Delphine moved through the room with a PR professional's bright efficiency, refilling coffee and redirecting any conversational thread that dared turn toward last night's revelation.

"The weather service says the roads should be passable by this afternoon," Delphine said. "Crews are already out. If anyone has urgent business in town—"

The radio in the adjoining butler's pantry cut her off.

It had been playing softly in the background—some innocuous jazz—but now a news bulletin broke in, the announcer's tone pitched toward urgency.

"—body of prominent New Orleans gallery owner and socialite Margot Devereux was discovered this morning—"

Camille's fork stopped halfway to her mouth.

"—at her Royal Street gallery in the French Quarter. Police are treating the death as suspicious. Devereux, who was acquitted three years ago in a high-profile art fraud case—"

Céleste moved quickly to turn the volume down, but it was too late. Everyone had heard.

The room had gone silent, all eyes turning to Camille.

"Well," Senator Mouton said with forced joviality. "That's quite a coincidence. Two deaths in two days, both connected to—" He seemed to realize what he was saying and stopped himself.

"Connected to Ms. Durant," Patricia Arceneaux finished for him, her voice cool and precise. "Marcus Kline on Friday. Margot Devereaux this morning. Both former clients. Both acquitted within the last few years." She looked at Camille with the expression of someone presenting evidence to a jury. "That's not coincidence. That's a pattern."

68

The radio murmured from the pantry, audible even at low volume.

"—no official comment yet on cause of death, but sources describe unusual markings at the scene and the presence of burned legal documents—"

"Burned legal documents," Patricia repeated, flat. "That's oddly specific."

"Coincidence?" Father Rousseau suggested quickly, crossing himself. "It's a tragedy. Two souls lost. We should pray for—"

"Two of them, in three days, with identical staging?" Patricia snapped. "Please."

"We should call the police," Vincent Thibodeaux said, his voice shaking. "This is—this isn't normal. This is—"

"This is none of our business," Adeline said, her voice cutting through the rising panic like a gavel. "These deaths occurred elsewhere, to people none of us knew personally, and while it's certainly distressing, there's no reason to believe they have anything to do with our gathering here."

"Except they were both represented by someone at this table," Patricia said.

All eyes on Camille again.

"I represented Ms. Devereux three years ago," Camille said, setting down her fork. "I haven't spoken to her since the case concluded. If the police believe there's a connection between these deaths, I'm sure they'll investigate appropriately."

"And if they find something?" Patricia pressed. "If there's evidence linking them?"

"Then I'll cooperate fully." Camille met her gaze. "As I'm sure we all would. Professional courtesy."

The tension hung in the air like humidity.

The silence broken with the chime of someone's phone with a news alert. Then another. Then a third. Everyone reached for their devices simultaneously.

Camille opened the notification on her screen.

SECOND SUSPICIOUS DEATH ROCKS LOUISIANA LEGAL COMMUNITY.

The article was short, sourced from the New Orleans police department's morning press briefing. Margot Devereaux, sixty-one, had been found by her assistant when the gallery opened that morning. Apparently heart failure. But—and here Camille's blood went cold—*investigators noted unusual markings at the scene, including symbols drawn in what appeared to be charcoal and the presence of burned legal documents.*

"But she's dead," Isabelle said quietly. She looked more tired than anyone else at the table, dark circles under her eyes. "And she died like Kline. Symbols. Burned papers. Tied to a case you won."

"That doesn't mean—" Camille began.

"It doesn't mean you killed them," Patricia cut in. "But it absolutely means someone is making a point about you."

"Or about the system," Vincent said. His voice shook. "About what happens when people like us"—he gestured vaguely around the table— "make things go away."

"'People like us,'" Isabelle repeated, bitter. "Nice euphemism."

Mireille had been quiet, sitting near the window with her coffee untouched. Now she spoke.

"Did the bulletin say where the markings were?" she asked. "On the walls? The floor? And what kind of symbols?"

"It doesn't say," Delphine answered, reading from her own screen. "But they're calling it 'ritualistic in nature.'"

"Don't," Céleste said sharply. "We don't need gory details over eggs."

"I do," Mireille said, voice mild. "Details matter. They tell you whether the working was careful or crude. Whether the scene is contrived to *look* ritualistic, or if in fact it *was*."

Adeline's gaze slid to her. "And what do the details tell you, Ms. Baptiste?"

"That whoever is doing this has a very specific sense of humor," Mireille said. "Legal documents burned as offerings. Hearts stopped in ways that look natural, but aren't. The symbols would make a difference, as would their placement. They'd have to be precise and specific." She glanced at Camille. "Three cases, most likely, if I'm correct. Three of your worst wins."

"There were only two," Camille said. "Kline and Devereux."

"Yes." Mireille's expression did not change. "For now."

The words settled over the table like a cloth.

"Oh for God's sake, Patricia muttered. "This is Louisiana. Every third death gets called 'ritualistic.' It's probably just —"

"Just what?" Isabelle asked, her voice tight. "Just a coincidence that two people died the same way in two days? Just random that they were both acquitted of serious crimes?" She turned to Camille. "Who's the third? Who else did you set free who went on to hurt people? What kind of deals id you make to win those cases?"

"Isabelle," Antoine said warningly.

"No!" The young woman stood, her chair scraping back. "Everyone's thinking it. Someone's targeting Ms. Durant's clients. Someone's killing people *she* got off. And we're all sitting here pretending it's normal!"

"Sit. Down," Adeline said quietly, with a punctuated forcefulness.

"Why? So we can keep pretending? So we can act like this house isn't—" She bit off whatever she was going to say, realizing she was pushing too hard. Pushing things too far.

Camille thought of the file on her credenza. The candlelight at the vigil. The boy in the Saints hoodie.

"Darryl James," she said. Saying his name aloud felt like dragging a stone up from deep water. "Vehicular homicide. Chemical leak. Dead employees. Families still waiting for justice."

"And you got him off," Isabelle said.

"I got him a plea and a suspended sentence on the original DUI," Camille said. "The chemical leak came later."

"And would the leak have happened if he'd been in prison?" Isabelle asked.

"Isabelle," Antoine said. "This isn't the time."

"When is the time?" she shot back.

"The time," Mireille said, "is now. Because whoever is doing this clearly understands the pattern better than you do. They've chosen Kline and Devereux not because they were your only ugly cases, but because they were part of a set. Three debts. Three corrections."

"Don't call them corrections," Father Rousseau said. "They're murders."

"It can be both, Father," Mireille said. "An act can be immoral and still respond to an imbalance."

"Enough," Adeline said. "We are not going to sit here and debate theology over breakfast. Whatever this is, we will let the authorities sort it."

"And what will you tell them," Camille asked, "when they ask why you invited me to Belle Rive the same weekend my clients started dropping like flies?"

Adeline's gaze sharpened. "I will tell them the truth, Ms. Durant. That it was a business retreat scheduled weeks ago. That you are one of my honored guest, not a suspect."

Delphine's phone buzzed. She checked it, frowned.

"Local news is already running with it," she said. "Kline and Devereux linked in the same segment. Speculation about a 'curse' on your clients, Camille."

"Of course," Camille said. "Why waste a perfectly good tragedy when you can brand it?"

"Camille," Mireille said quietly. "When was the last time you heard from James?"

"A few weeks ago," Camille said. "His new counsel wanted access to my old files for the environmental investigation. I declined. Conflict issues."

"Have you tried reaching him since all this started?" Mireille asked.

"No," Camille said. "Why would I?"

"Because if the pattern holds," Mireille said, "he's next."

Another painfully long silence hung in the air.

Senator Mouton cleared his throat. "We're all getting ahead of ourselves. Two tragic deaths do *not* a serial case make. No need to jump to conclusions."

"Tell that to your voters," Delphine said. "They love patterns. And scapegoats."

"Then find a better one than me," Camille said.

No one volunteered.

Outside, rain began again in a thin, needling drizzle, tapping against the windows like impatient fingers.

Two deaths. Two debts. Two lines in an invisible ledger marked paid.

The third line, Camille knew, had already been drawn.

It was just waiting for ink.

Chapter 7.5
Exhibit A: Margot Devereaux

The first time Margot Devereaux took the stand, the courtroom felt like it was humoring her. She moved through the well as if it were a runway, all sharp collarbones and immaculate black dress, dark hair swept into a knot that probably had a name. The jurors watched her the way people watched gallery openings—half admiration, half suspicion they were being sold something they didn't quite understand.

State v. Devereaux. Art fraud, wire fraud, theft by deception. A tidy list of counts wrapped in expensive paper. The state's theory was simple: Margot had used her boutique gallery to sell "lost" works by mid-century Louisiana painters, accompanied by forged provenance and forged appraisals. Elderly collectors, trust fund kids, a small museum in Lafayette—they'd all bought what she was selling.

Camille had read the file twice before she agreed to take it. The evidence was, on paper, robust: emails, bank trails, a seized storage unit full of suspiciously fresh canvases. But Margot had money, and Margot had hired her, and in those days that still meant something uncomplicated in Camille's mind. Everyone deserved a defense. Even the ones who took pleasure in the con.

"You understand," Margot had said in their first meeting, sitting in Camille's office like she owned the furniture, "provenance is a story. Stories get revised. That doesn't make them lies. It makes them...adaptive."

"What you're accused of is a bit more than revision," Camille had replied. "You sold work as original when it wasn't."

Margot had smiled, slow and feline. "Everyone got exactly what they wanted, Ms. Durant. Beautiful objects. A sense of importance. Validation. The only thing they didn't get was the ability to profit from its later resale. I removed the speculation. That's a kindness in this market."

Camille had filed that away as "jury poison" and steered the conversation back to the search warrant.

The state's case hinged on that warrant. A mid-level investigator had walked into Margot's storage unit on a tip, seen too many paintings with suspiciously similar signatures, and gone back for legal cover. The warrant application read thin even on a first pass—conclusory language, vague references to "confidential informants," no independent corroboration—but the judge had signed it, and the search had yielded everything the DA needed to build a pretty narrative.

On cross, Camille made the narrative ugly.

"In your affidavit," she said to the investigator, sliding the photocopy onto the rail, "you state under oath that you had

78

'substantial reason to believe' the works in Ms. Devereaux's possession were forgeries. Could you define 'substantial' for the jury?"

The man shifted. "I—I meant I had strong suspicions, based on my training."

"Suspicion is not, to my knowledge, a legal standard," Camille said pleasantly. "What, specifically, did you rely on?"

He pointed to the tip, to vague comments from "industry insiders," to the fact that Margot's inventory had grown quickly.

"Did you commission an independent expert before applying for the warrant?"

"No."

"Did you attempt to purchase a painting undercover, to see if Ms. Devereaux misrepresented it to you personally?"

"No."

"So, to be clear, the only 'substantial' basis you had was that someone you won't name told you something you didn't verify, and a successful businesswoman was...too successful for your comfort."

Hargrove, the prosecutor, objected. Camille rephrased. The judge's frown deepened at the word confidential every time it appeared. Jurors scribbled notes. She pressed on.

Later, in chambers, she argued the chain that started with that warrant tainted everything that followed. Fruit of the poisonous tree. The judge was not inclined to toss a whole case on what he called "technical shortcomings" in the paperwork. But Camille knew how to sharpen a shortcoming into a blade.

"This isn't a typo, Your Honor," she said. "It's a fishing expedition blessed after the fact. If we allow warrants built on uncorroborated gossip, every private cache in this parish is fair game. That is not how we do law, and you know it."

He'd looked at the affidavit again, thumb smoothing the crease where his clerk had folded it. A small furrow appeared between his brows.

"I'm not throwing the whole case out," he said at last. "But the storage unit search is excluded. Anything that came from that is inadmissible."

Hargrove had gone red. "That's the bulk of the evidence, Your Honor."

"Then perhaps the state should be more careful when it asks permission to kick in doors," the judge said as he gaveled them back to order.

Camille had felt the shift in the room as the ruling filtered back to counsel table—the way the jurors sat forward, the way Margot's shoulders relaxed a fraction. From there, the state's case bled out slowly. Without the seized inventory, what remained were unhappy buyers and circumstantial trails that could be framed as sour grapes. Margot didn't have to testify. Camille made sure she didn't.

In the hallway afterward, Hargrove confronted her near the elevators. "You just let a thief walk."

"I prevented a bad warrant from becoming precedent," she replied. "If you can't tell the difference, that's your problem, not mine."

Privately, she knew there was a difference and that it wasn't as clean as she wanted it to be. But the law had rules. She'd played by them and won. That was supposed to be the end of the story.

It wasn't.

Four months later, Margot invited her to a private reception at the gallery. "As thanks," the card had read, looping handwriting on thick cream stock. "For saving my life."

Camille almost didn't go. Work was busy, her calendar brutal. But curiosity, as it always did, outweighed better judgment. She told herself it was networking.

The gallery was all white walls and curated light, jazz low over hidden speakers. Soft laughter, clink of glass. Margaret Devereaux glided toward her with a flute of champagne and a kiss near her cheek.

"You came," Margot said. "I'm flattered."

"You were very insistent," Camille said. "And my office is close."

"Still a romantic," Margot murmured. "Come, let me show you something."

She steered Camille toward a back room, away from the main show. Smaller space, less polished, canvases stacked in racks. The air smelled of oil and turpentine, less antiseptic than the front-of-house.

"These are the ones that matter," Margot said. "The patrons in there," she flicked a hand toward the laughter, "they want names. I want stories."

She pulled out a canvas—a storm over a cane field, all bruised grays and violent motion. It was stunning, even to Camille's untrained eye.

"It's beautiful," Camille said.

"It's anonymous," Margot corrected, amusement in her voice. "The artist died ten years ago. No reputation, no auction record. I can hang it with a made-up biography and watch the price triple. Do you think anyone will care, as long as it photographs well?"

There was a bitterness under the silk that Camille hadn't heard before. It scraped against her memory of victims on the stand, their quiet humiliation.

"Do you ever think about the people you sold to?" Camille asked.

"Afterward?"

"Of course," Margot said. "I think about whether they enjoy what they hung on their walls. The rest is the market's problem."

Camille thought of the Lafeyette museum's director on cross, voice shaking as he described cutting educational programs to cover the loss. She thought of an elderly couple, fingers knotted together, saying they'd have to sell their house.

"You told the court everyone got exactly what they paid for," she said.

"And they did," Margot said. "They paid for a feeling. Authenticity is a story. Lawyers should understand that better than anyone."

For a moment, Camille saw herself through Margot's eyes— another artisan of narrative, dressing outcomes in legitimacy. It left a film on her tongue.

She left early, citing a morning hearing. On the sidewalk outside, the night was heavy and damp, the city humming around her. A block away, beneath a flickering streetlamp, a woman in a Saints hoodie stood studying a gallery flyer, lips pressed thin.

"We saved her," Camille's boss had said when the verdict came in. "Kept government overreach in check. The market will sort itself out."

The market, looking at Margot's new champagne, didn't seem inclined to correct anything.

Months later, when Margot's name appeared in a brief mention about "ongoing civil suits" and "private settlements," Camille read to the end of the article, then closed her browser and pushed the thought away. The law had done what it was supposed to do. She had done what she was paid to do.

Somewhere, a ledger line had been written:

> *DEVEREAUX, MARGOT – verdict adjusted.*
> *Consequences deferred.*

At Belle Rive, with two of the three dead and their aftermaths splashed across the news, that deferred column was finally coming due. Margot Devereaux had never been just a name on the crawl. She was Exhibit A.

Chapter 8

Investigation Begins

Belle Rive was full of lies, and every room was uncomfortable.

By midday, Camille had done enough pacing to map Belle Rive's ground floor by sound alone. The house was starting to feel familiar in the worst way—like a courtroom you'd spent too many days in, down to the echo of certain corners.

It was one thing to know, in the abstract, that someone might be hunting your clients.

It was very much another to walk through a house full of people who all might have handed them the knife.

She forced herself into work mode. Work had a process–it had rules. Work was simple.

Step one: interviews.

Camille had questioned dozens of witnesses in her career. She knew how to read a room, how to spot lies, how to make someone uncomfortable enough to tell the truth just to fill the silence.

She started in the conservatory, where the humid air and lush greenery made her feel like she was being watched, and pressed, from all sides.

Vincent Thibodeaux sat at a small table among the potted palms. He was ostensibly reading a newspaper but really just staring at the same page while his coffee went cold. When Camille sat down across from him, he flinched as though she'd fired a gun.

"Mr. Thibodeaux," Camille said, "I'd like to ask you a few questions."

He flinched like she'd said "indictment."

"I already told you, Ms. Durant, I don't know anything about occult symbols," he said. "I develop properties. I don't draw chalk circles in basements."

"I'm not asking about chalk circles," she said. "I'm asking about connections. You knew Marcus Kline. You met Margot Devereux. How close were you to either of them really?"

"Kline was…a partner on a couple of projects," Vincent said. "We went to the same charity dinners. Spoke the same language. Devereux I only met once at an opening. I didn't particularly care for her."

"Why?"

"She reminded me of me," he said. "Only as a female and with better clothes."

He tried to smile. Failed.

"You said last night you knew what this weekend was," Camille said. "That you knew what Adeline wanted. What did you mean?"

Vincent stared at his hands. "Look around you," he said softly. "Everyone here has eaten at this table before. Some of us came when we needed money. Some when we needed permits. Some when we needed certain files to go missing or certain people to forget what they saw. No one comes to Belle Rive for the scenery."

"You came for—"

"A zoning issue." He laughed once, without humor. "That's how it starts. You need a variance. You need a signature. You find out who whispers in whose ear. And then, if you're smart—or stupid—you find your way here. My first project— the one that made my career—I *never* should have gotten the permits. The environmental review alone should have killed it. But Adeline knew someone. She made a call. And suddenly all my problems went away."

"In exchange for—"

" A percentage. Future Favors. The understanding that when the LeBlancs needed something, I'd deliver." He laughed bitterly. "I thought it was just business. Just how things worked at this level in this town. I had no idea—"

"And then?"

"And then someone like Adeline introduces you to someone like Patricia. Or someone at the state. Or someone in a little room with candles who says your project could use a bit of...luck."

"Did anyone ever introduce you to Mireille?" Camille asked.

Vincent shook his head. "No. I didn't know her name until last night. But I've heard rumors. About women who can tilt a judge's mood, or send a key witness home with a sudden illness." He met Camille's eyes. "Like what happened in your James case."

Her stomach tightened.

"You think that was magic," she said.

"I think it was...convenient," he replied. "And convenience is never free."

"Do you owe anyone here?" she asked.

"I owe *everyone* here," he said. "That's the problem." He put his head in his hands, "Jesus. My wife wanted us to come this weekend. I thought better of it, but she insisted that it would be good for business. Good for connections. She just doesn't know. She doesn't understand what this family is. What they're tied to."

"And what exactly are they?" Camille pressed.

He just shook his head, tongue-tied and oozing with regret.

She waited a moment, then stood. "If you remember anything more concrete than rumors and insinuation—invoices, emails, anything that suggests someone's been orchestrating this—you need to tell me."

"And if the someone is here? In this house with us?" he asked.

"Especially then," she said.

He didn't look reassured.

****

She found Patricia Arceneaux in Adeline's study, surrounded by neat stacks of paper. The older woman looked up from a ledger as Camille entered, expression cool.

"Ms. Durant," Patricia said. "To what do I owe the pleasure?"

"Let's save ourselves some time." Camille stepped closer. "Professional to professional, why does Claude LeBlanc's archive contain detailed notes on cases corrected by Émiline Baptiste?"

Patricia's fingers stilled. The only betrayal.

"You've been in the archive," she said.

"Yes," Camille said. "Mireille took me. I saw *State v. Devereux, Claude.* Sylvie Baptiste. Practicing attorney: you. Practitioner: Émiline Baptiste. Correction: one car accident on the Causeway."

Patricia closed the ledger with care. "If you're trying to provoke a confession, you'll need to do better than innuendo and half facts."

"I'm trying to understand why a paralegal-turned-practitioner with a grudge has been following *my* career," Camille said. "And why *your name* keeps popping up in the margins of her early work."

"Émiline was a clerk," Patricia said. "I won that Devereux case on a suppression motion. Legally. Whatever happened to him afterward had nothing to do with me."

"Except you kept working with the people who hired her," Camille said. "Claude. Adeline. The family who saw that magic worked and thought, 'Excellent, another tool.'"

Patricia smiled thinly. "And you haven't?"

"I didn't even know magic was on the table," Camille said.

"Didn't you?" Patricia's head tilted. "Every time a piece of evidence went missing at exactly the right moment? Every time a judge suddenly granted a motion you never expected? You never once thought, *something* is helping me?"

"I thought I was good at my job," Camille said.

"You're arrogant, but yes, you're good at your job." Patricia's gaze sharpened. "That's why they like you. Why they invited you into this little weekend crucible. They want to see if you're smart enough to survive it."

"Am I?" Camille asked.

"Jury's out," Patricia said. "Literal and metaphorical."

Camille glanced at the papers on the desk. "What are you working on?"

"Damage control." Patricia tapped a folder. "Messaging for when the archive inevitably comes to light. Arguments for why certain documents are privileged. Strategies to frame these deaths as tragic aberration rather than the inevitable outcome of systemic rot."

"So you're already anticipating exposure," Camille said.

"I live in anticipation," Patricia replied. "It's my job."

"Is it also your job to decide who gets corrected?" Camille asked. "Were you the one who handed Émiline my cases? Kline. Devereux. James."

"No," Patricia said. "If I'd been choosing, I'd have started with worse men."

"Like who?" Camille pressed.

For a heartbeat, something like real anger flashed across Patricia's face. Then it was gone.

"Leave my ghosts alone, Ms. Durant," she said. "You have enough of your own. If you're looking for a killer, look at the person with he most to gain from destroying your reputation. Who benefits most from you being seen as someone whose clients die mysteriously? Someone who profits from you being investigated, discredited, and removed from the board?"

Camille didn't have an answer.

Patricia smiled coldly. "When you figure that out, let me know. Until then, I'd appreciate if you didn't interrupt my work."

Dismissed.

****

Outside, the clouds thickened again. A faint roll of thunder.

She found Isabelle LeBlanc in the side garden, cigarette cupped in her hand against the drizzle, saying she wished the system actually hurt people who deserved it instead of their victims and staring at something Camille couldn't see.

"Isabelle?"

She turned, her eyes red from crying. "Did you know? When you defended them? Did you know what they would do after?"

Camille approached carefully, like Isabell was a startled deer. "Did I know they were guilty? Yes. But no, I didn't know what would happen next. That's not something—"

"It should be." Her voice was fierce, unexpected. "You should have to know. Should have to look at the photographs of the people they killed and say 'yes, I helped this happen.' You should have to carry it."

"I do."

"Not nearly enough. Because in spite of it all, you continue to do what you do." Isabelle turned back to the garden. "My grandmother built this family on blood. My great-grandfather seized land after the war, pushed people off their land, destroyed lives to build his fortune. And every generation since has done the same. Different methods, same sin. Repeatedly. And people like you, Ms. Durant, continue to make it possible."

"I'm not responsible for—"

"You're responsible for exactly what you did. You took their blood money. You used your skills to pervert justice. And you told yourself it was fine because everyone deserves a defense." Isabelle's laugh was harsh. "That's what they all say. The lawyers, the fixers, the consultants. Everyone's 'just doing their job.' Nobody's actually responsible for the consequences."

Camille felt the words hit home, felt the truth in them like a knife between her ribs.

"I'm trying to stop it," she said quietly. "The killings. I'm trying to figure out who's doing this."

Isabelle stood up. "maybe you should let them finish. Maybe some debts deserve to be paid."

She walked past Camille back toward the house, leaving her footprints to gradually disappear on the muddy path.

****

Camille spent the rest of the afternoon moving through the house, collecting fragments.

Father Rousseau in the chapel-like sitting room, insisting that vengeance belonged to God while looking very much like he wanted to reserve the right to help.

Étienne on the phone, voice low, telling someone in New York that "the situation is contained, for now," and that "Mother will handle the optics."

Each conversation added weight to the sense that she was walking through the aftermath of a crime in progress.

Not just the killings.

The years of quiet deals that had made them possible.

Near dusk, as she stood in an upstairs corridor watching rain snake down the glass, her phone buzzed.

Detective Broussard.

She answered. "Detective."

"Ms. Durant." Broussard sounded tired and more wary than hostile. "You still at Belle Rive?"

"Yes."

"Figured as much," he said. "Look, I won't waste your time. We're trying to locate one of your former clients."

"Which one?"

"Darryl James."

Her fingers tightened on the phone. "What's happened?"

"That's what I'd like to know," Broussard said. "He missed a scheduled meeting with his counsel yesterday. No one's seen him since late afternoon. His office says he left in a hurry before the worst of the storm hit, said something about 'getting out of town for a few days.' No one's heard from him since."

"Have you checked his home?" Camille asked.

"Housekeeper says he never came back last night," Broussard said. "His car's not in the drive. We're checking traffic cams along the Causeway and near the lake. With the weather, a lot of footage is useless."

"Do you think—" She stopped. The word *dead* felt heavy in her mouth.

"I think," Broussard said slowly, "that given what happened to Kline and Devereux, I can't treat this like a harmless midlife crisis road trip. I think if someone is targeting your clients, he's likely on that list. And I think if you know anything that could help me find him before that happens, now would be the time."

"I don't," she said. "I haven't spoken to him in weeks. His current counsel requested access to my case notes. I refused."

"Why?" Broussard asked.

"Because I didn't want to be back in his orbit," she said. "Because I thought if I kept an arm's length from whatever mess he'd made, it wouldn't be my problem."

"How's that working out for you?" Broussard asked.

"Spectacularly," she said.

He exhaled. "All right. If you hear from him, you call me. Immediately. And Ms. Durant?"

"Yes?"

"Keep your head down," he said. "If this is about you, you're not just a vector. You're likely a target too."

He hung up.

Camille lowered the phone slowly.

Somewhere between Belle Rive and New Orleans, a man whose freedom she'd preserved was moving through the dark, unaccounted for.

The current, she thought, had an excellent sense of timing.

She had the sudden, irrational urge to drive to the lake, to stand by the water and wait for headlights.

Instead, she turned away from the window and went looking for Mireille.

The witch would understand what it meant when the third name on a list started to flicker.

Chapter 9
Flashbacks & Archives

amille needed clarity. She got flashbacks instead.

They came not as streams but as slides of memory projected against the inside of her skull as she walked.

Marcus Kline's face, rapturous with relief outside the courthouse.

Margot Devereaux's poised disdain on the stand, that little smile when the judge ruled key evidence as inadmissible.

Darryl James's hand on her arm as they waited for the jury, his grip a fraction too familiar. "You're saving my life," he'd whispered. "I won't forget it."

She remembered looking down at her legal pad and realizing she'd been tracing a pattern—a looped, balanced symbol she didn't recognize.

Had she drawn it? Or had someone guided her hand?

"Helpful, aren't they?" a voice asked.

She'd reached the back staircase without realizing it. Mireille stood on the landing above, watching her.

"Flashbacks," Mireille added. "Not the most comfortable bool, but effective. The current is reminding you what you agreed to."

"I never agreed to this."

"You agreed to outcomes," she said. "You wanted wins. The current isn't sentimental. It doesn't care whether you know the terms."

"Then why show me these scenes now?"

"So you don't lie to yourself when we go into the archive."

Camille frowned. "Archive?"

Mireille smiled without warmth. "You really thought a house like this wouldn't have one?"

She turned and continued up the back stairs. Camille followed.

The archive door was the kind of door you didn't notice unless you knew to look for it—tucked behind a linen closet in the east wing, painted the same dull white as the wall. No plaque. No label. No handle.

"Claude liked things that could be hidden in plain sight," Mireille said, producing an old brass key she had produced from somewhere within her dress and turning it in the lock. "Adeline prefers them buried. This room is the compromise."

The lock yielded with a reluctant click.

The air inside was cool and dry, courtesy of a portable unit humming softly in the corner. Shelves lined the walls from floor to ceiling, overloaded with boxes and ledgers. A long table ran down the center of the room, its surface crowded with open files.

It looked like a clerk's office that had been abandoned in the middle of a busy day and then carefully preserved.

"What is this?" Camille asked.

"Memory," Mireille said. "Weaponized."

She stepped inside, motioned for Camille to follow.

"Claude started this system in the late eighties," Mireille went on. "He believed in paper trails. Not because he respected the law, but because he respected leverage. This was the LeBlanc family insurance policy, as it were. Records of favors, debts, gifts, bribes. Every check that was ever quietly rerouted, every zoning exception, every unreported donation."

She ran her fingers along the nearest shelf, tracing the handwritten labels.

MOUTON – DONATIONS. CITY CONTRACTS – RIVERBEND. ARCADIA DEVELOPMENT – PERMITS.

"And here," she said, stopping at a box on a lower shelf, "is the part that interests us. More recently," she went on," someone added a new kind of file."

The label on the front was printed, not handwritten.

DURANT.

"Of course," Camille murmured.

She lifted the lid.

On top lay a manila folder with her bar photo clipped to the inside flap. Her law school transcripts. Early case summaries. Press clippings:

> YOUNG DEFENSE ATTORNEY WINS IMPOSSIBLE CASE. DURANT STRIKES AGAIN.

"Flattering," she said dryly.

"Keep going," Mireille said.

Beneath the general material were individual folders, each tabbed with a client's name.

KLINE, MARCUS. DEVEREUX, MARGOT. JAMES, DARRYL. Others she recognized. Others she'd almost forgotten.

Each file contained:

- A summary of the original charges and verdict.
- Notes on anomalies in the proceedings: witnesses who recanted, evidence that disappeared, judges who had sudden changes of heart.
- Clippings of later news articles, cataloging what each

client did after walking out of court.

In the margins, in a small, slanted hand, someone had scribbled comments.

- *Key witness collapsed on stand. Intervention successful.*
- *Chain of custody "lost." Court accepted argument with minimal resistance.*
- *Press outraged. Public perception: injustice.*

"Who wrote these?" Camille asked.

"My cousin, Émiline," Mireille said. "At least at first. When she started helping Claude and his friends...tidy up."

"Helping," Camille echoed.

"Helping the current find places where a little push would have big downstream effects," Mireille said. "Helping tidy the books. She thought she was just balancing. She didn't understand how many people were using her work for profit."

Camille's eye caught on a symbol in one margin—a set of barely sketched scales, one side heavily inked.

"Is that—"

"The current's shorthand for 'debt outstanding,'" Mireille said. "She picked it up from older ledgers."

"How long has this been going on?" Camille whispered.

"Long enough." Mireille closed the box Camille flipped to the back of the Durant file.

Mirielle pointed toward the far wall where a separate, older cabinet sat. It looked like it had been salvaged from a courthouse—heavy oak, brass handles. The drawers were labeled with years.

"Adeline didn't have this installed," Mireille said. "Her husband did. Claude like records. And he liked leverage. When he discovered the family's...other patronage stream, he started documenting that too."

She opened the drawer marked 1998-2002.

Inside were files that looked different from the others.

Thinner. Each with two names: a defendant and a victim. Beneath those, in that same slanted hand, a third name: *practitioner*.

Camille pulled one at random.

State v. Devereux, Claude. Victim: Sylvie Baptiste. Practitioner: É. Baptiste. Correction: auto collision, Causeway Bridge.

State v. Hollis. Victim: multiple investors. Practitioner: É. Baptiste. Correction: heart failure, hotel room.

There were more than a dozen files like this.

"She's been at this a long time," Camille said.

"She learned from the best," Mireille replied. "Or the worst. Depending on your point of view."

"And Claude knew," Camille added. Knew she was killing people and kept records of it.

"He likely thought it made him safe," Mireille said. "As long as the practitioner was useful to him, he had no reason to stop her. And if she ever turned on him, he could expose her. Leverage, chère. Your favorite word."

"So this is where it started," Mireille said.

"And this," Camille said, gesturing to the Durant box, "is where it...evolved."

"Yes," Mireille said. "Once Claude realized you were particularly blessed with improbable outcomes, he started tracking you separately. You became a somewhat of a pet project, you could say."

There, on a single page, was a list of her major cases. Each had one of three notations:

- *Assistance requested.*
- *Assistance offered.*
- *No intervention.*

Some had checkmarks. Others had small symbols she was beginning to recognize.

At the bottom were three names written in darker ink, underlined.

KLINE, MARCUS – *paid in full.*
DEVEREUX, MARGOT – *paid in full.*
JAMES, DARRYL – *balance pending.*

"Pending," she said. The word lodged behind her ribs. "Not paid."

"Not yet," Mireille said. "But if the pattern holds, someone is working very hard to change that status."

"Someone in this house," Camille said. "They have my files. They have these notes. They have access to these archives and know exactly which three cases cut deepest."

"Yes," Mireille said. "And they know that once James's line reads *paid in full,* they'll have completed a working years in the making."

"Why three?" Camille asked.

"Threes sit well with the current," Mireille said. "Past, present, future. Crime, verdict, consequence. Three cases where the law failed spectacularly make a neat offering."

"Neat," Camille repeated, choking on it.

She flipped to another section of the file. There, at the very bottom, alone on a page, was her own name.

DURANT, CAMILLE – *balance outstanding.*

Her fingers went cold.

"What does that mean?" she asked, though she knew.

"It means," Mireille said gently, "that in the current's eyes, these three deaths don't clear *you*. They clear the accounts on Kline, Devereux, James. Your account remains open."

"You mean this isn't about punishing them," Camille said. "It's about punishing me."

"It's about correcting the harm your wins enabled," Mireille said. "But yes. Whoever is doing this chose you as the axis. They could have gone after any number of attorneys. They chose the one Claude flagged as a...how did he put it?" Her mouth twisted. "A 'promising asset.'"

"Does Adeline know this is here?" Camille asked.

"She knows he kept records," Mireille said. "She may not know how detailed they are. Or how much he leaned on my cousin."

A noise in the hall made them both still. Footsteps, quick, then gone.

"Someone's been down here recently," Camille said, taking in the disturbed dust on the table, the files left open.

"Yes," Mireille said. "The architect."

"Émiline," Camille said.

"Or her handler," Mireille said.

Camille looked up sharply. "You think there's someone else."

"I know Émiline," Mireille said. "She's brilliant and dangerous, but she's not subtle in this way. Someone here is curating her targets. Feeding her information. Using her crusade to settle mundane scores."

"And all of that," Camille said, "is stacked on top of what I did in court before anyone whispered to a spirit."

"Correct," Mireille said. "The current isn't sentimental. It doesn't care whether the imbalance came from law, money, or magic. It just wants the ledger to even out."

"And what does it want from me?" Camille asked.

"That," Mireille said, closing the lid on the box, "is what we still have to ask it."

The lights flickered. Once, twice. The hum of the cooling unit wavered and steadied.

"The house knows we're here," Mireille said. "Time to go before whoever uses this room does their own inventory."

They left the archive as they'd found it, the door clicking shut behind them, leaving paper and ink and years of secrets in the cool dark.

But the knowledge had shifted.

And in a house like Belle Rive, knowledge was the most dangerous currency of all.

In Camille's mind, the words "balance pending" burned like a verdict not yet read.

Chapter 9.5
Archive: The One That Broke Her

Émiline Baptiste had been a clerk for seven years when she learned the current could bite back.

It was a hot August, the kind where the air in the courthouse basement hung thick and unmoving. *State v. Landry*. Cop on trial for excessive force—beating a handcuffed suspect into a coma during a traffic stop. Video blurry but damning, witness statements stacking against him. Landry was old guard, connected, the kind of badge who golfed with the DA's brother. His attorney was good, but the evidence was better.

Émiline had watched the arraignment from the back. The victim's family in the gallery—mother clutching a rosary, brother with eyes like chipped flint. Imbalance screamed from the room: blue wall closing ranks, truth bent to protect its own.

That night, in her tiny walk-up off Rampart, Émiline prepared. No grand circle, no chanting. The current wasn't theater. She laid out Landry's booking photo, a printout of the dash cam log, a vial of rainwater from the precinct steps. Candles for the four corners. Her scales pendant, heavy at her throat.

"Balance," she whispered, dripping wax on the photo's eyes. "Not the law's. The victim's."

The hum came quick—chest-deep, river current pulling under. She fed it specifics: the family's grief, Landry's smirk on intake, the coma kid's name. Intent sharp as a plea bargain.

Next day, trial day three. Landry's cross of the victim's brother went south—sudden nosebleed mid-answer, paramedics called. Jury unsettled. DA smelled blood.

Then the dash cam footage. Tech guy cued it up. Screen flickered. Audio crackled. Video... froze on Landry's raised baton. No forward motion. Just that frame, looped.

"Technical glitch," tech stammered.

Hargrove erupted. Defense pounced—tampered evidence, reasonable doubt. Judge declared mistrial.

Émiline filed the dismissal paperwork herself, hands steady. Balance restored.

Except it wasn't.

Two weeks later: news alert. Victim's brother—witness, the one with the nosebleed—dead. Car wreck on I-10. Single occupant, no drugs, no alcohol. Brakes failed. Mechanic: "Tampered line. Clean cut."

Émiline stared at the screen, mug cold in her hand. The current had taken the wrong debt.

She drove to the crash site that night, scales burning at her throat. Highway shoulder littered with glass petals, faded flowers from passersby. She stood in the dark, rain starting, and whispered the rite backward—release, unbind, correct.

Nothing hummed. No answer.

Back home, she pored over her own ledger. Landry walked free. Victim still comatose. Brother dead—innocent variable, collateral in the flow. Scales tilted wrong: cop safe, family shattered worse.

Claude LeBlanc called next morning. "Heard about Landry. Clean work. Name your price."

Émiline gripped the phone. "Wrong line snapped."

Silence. Then: "Adjust the math next time. Patterns hold."

She did. Started documenting—variables, intents, outcomes. Threes for stability. Intent over accident. Ledgers grew precise, rigid. The current forgave sloppiness once. Not twice.

Years later, reviewing Camille Durant's file by candlelight, Émiline traced the scales. Patterns prevented breaks. Three cases, clean. No collaterals.

But Mireille's warning echoed: *Wins rot.*

Émiline closed the ledger. Rot was the world's problem. Balance was hers.

Chapter 10

A Third Death

They didn't need the radio or a television this time.

By late afternoon, the house itself had become a relay station. Phones chimed with alerts; laptops glowed with new footage; the staff passed whispers along the corridors like contraband.

The guests gathered in the drawing room again, as if drawn by the gravitational pull of collective dread.

On the muted TV, an anchor stood by a stretch of highway slick with rain. Behind her, emergency vehicles clustered around the twisted remains of a car wrapped around a utility pole, emergency lights strobing red and blue against the rain-slick pavement. The chyron read:

THIRD FORMER CLIENT OF DEFENSE ATTORNEY CAMILLE DURANT FOUND DEAD.

Someone had sent that word in early. They always did.

"—authorities are hesitant to comment on specifics, but have confirmed that the victim has been identified as local businessman and industrialist Darryl James," the anchor was saying. "James was at the center of ongoing investigations into a chemical leak in St. James Parish that left multiple workers dead and dozens ill. He was also previously acquitted in a controversial DUI case involving multiple fatalities."

A photo of James appeared beside her—a PR shot, smiling, suit crisp, eyes confident.

Beside it, a smaller image: a courtroom still. Camille at counsel table, hair pulled back, expression composed, James at her side.

Camille felt the floor tilt under her feet.

"Mute it," Adeline said.

Delphine obeyed. The room filled with silence and flashing images instead of sound.

"...is that—" Vincent began.

"Yes," Camille said. Her voice sounded odd in her own ears. "It's him."

On the screen, the anchor continued to talk over B-roll: police tape flapping in the wind, a white sheet being lifted onto a gurney, close-ups of skid marks disappearing into standing water.

Text crawled along the bottom:

UNUSUAL SYMBOLS FOUND INSIDE VEHICLE, SOURCES SAY, ALONG WITH BURNED LEGAL DOCUMENTS

"Same pattern," Patricia said quietly.

"Three cases," Mireille murmured. "Three corrections. Neat little set."

"Stop calling them that," Isabelle said sharply. "They're executions."

"Executions can be corrective," Mireille said. "That's what makes them so tempting."

Senator Mouton swallowed audibly. "This is...this is going to be bad. For the state. For all of us."

"For me," Camille said.

The screen shifted to stock footage of her walking up courthouse steps, microphones thrust toward her. The anchor's voice, though muted, was clearly saying her name.

"I need to turn this off," Céleste said. "For everyone's sanity."

"Leave it," Adeline said. "We should see what story they're telling."

Camille watched herself, years younger, fit into the same box as James and Kline and Devereux.

"Three of her clients," Isabelle said. "Three in three days. How is that not a sign?"

"Of what?" Antoine asked. "That she's cursed? That someone's trying to frame her? That God finally got bored with subtlety?"

"That the system failed," Isabelle said. "Over and over. And someone decided to fix it."

"By killing people," Vincent said. "Let's not romanticize this."

"Whoever is doing this isn't just killing," Patricia said. "They're staging. Sending a message. And they chose you as the messenger, Ms. Durant. They're pinning their thesis to your chest."

"Stop." Adeline's tone left no room for argument. "We will *not* eat each other alive in my house. Whatever is happening out there, we will deal with it. Together."

"Together?" Senator Mouton's laugh was brittle. "With all due respect, Adeline, we are not a monolith. Some of us have elections to worry about. Some of us have donors. Some of us would prefer *not* to be photographed walking out of a plantation house in the middle of a serial killer investigation."

"Then by all means," Adeline said cooly, "feel free to wade through the mud and see how far you get before *your* car sinks."

Mouton shut his mouth.

Camille stood with her back to the wall, watching the currents move—fear, calculation, resentment. The archive still echoed in her head: files, names, balances marked paid. Hers, marked outstanding.

She should have felt relief that the pattern had completed without touching anyone at Belle Rive.

She felt anything but.

"This isn't just about me," she said.

"Oh?" Patricia raised an eyebrow. "Three bodies might disagree."

"This is about whoever compiled that archive upstairs," Camille went on, ignoring her. "Whoever has been tracking my cases, deciding where the current should intervene."

Mireille, perched in an armchair by the window, gave the faintest tilt of her head.

"Archive?" Delphine repeated. "What archive?"

Adeline's gaze snapped to Camille. Just for a moment, the mask slipped, and Camille saw it: she knew. Or at least suspected.

"You've been exploring my house," Adeline said.

"You invited me into your house as a problem solver," Camille replied. "I found a problem."

"And what precisely did you find?"

"Records," Camille said. "Boxes of them. Files on your deals, your favors, your clients. And a box on me."

The room tightened.

"You should have told me if you were going to snoop," Adeline said.

"You should have told me if you were going to file my soul under D."

A flicker of amusement crossed Adeline's face, there and gone. "Everyone in this room has a file somewhere," she said. "You don't keep people in line with charm alone."

"I saw more than leverage," Camille said. "I saw a pattern. Your late husband knew about a practitioner correcting cases where the law failed. He kept records of those, too. And someone has been continuing that work. My cases are just the latest entries."

Patricia's composure slipped for the first time. "You're accusing a dead man of conspiracy with a serial killer?"

"I'm saying he understood that magic was just another tool," Camille said. "And someone in this house learned that lesson very well."

"You're out of line," Patricia snapped.

"It's a legitimate question," Vincent said quietly. He'd been silent until now, absorbing, watching. "If someone here has been...directing this, don't we have a right to know? Especially if we're being used as alibis."

"Alibis for what?" Senator Mouton demanded. "We've all been here. None of us could have killed these people personally—"

"The workings don't require proximity," Mireille said. "Not once the link is established. Once you have the right objects, the right knowledge, you can set the pattern and let the current carry it where it will."

"So someone here could have pulled the trigger from this house," Isabelle said. "Good to know."

Camille's phone buzzed again. Another call from Broussard. She excused herself, stepping into the hall to answer.

"Detective."

"Ms. Durant." Broussard sounded more tired than accusatory now. "We've got the preliminary from the James scene. Same symbols. Same burned paperwork. And…"

"And?" she prompted.

"And something new." He hesitated. "We found a photograph of you in the glove compartment. Your business card stapled to it. Someone wanted to make sure we knew this was about you."

Her hand tightened around the phone until her knuckles ached.

"That's not subtle," she said.

"I'm past subtle," Broussard said. "So, apparently, is whoever's doing this. Whether or not you had anything to do with these deaths, this is now officially your problem. My superiors want me to treat you as a potential target *and* a potential suspect."

"Those are mutually exclusive categories, Detective," she said.

"Not these days," he replied. "I'm coming out to Belle Rive later with a team to secure certain records. I've heard rumors about an archive."

She thought of the room behind the linen closet. The files. Her name.

"Rumors travel fast," she said.

"In this state, they always have," Broussard said. "Can you do something for me, Ms. Durant?"

"That depends."

"When I get there," he said, "don't stonewall me. Don't lawyer me. Don't hide behind privilege or spin. If you want me to believe you're not orchestrating this, help me find who is."

She hesitated.

"I'll show you what I can," she said.

"Make it enough," he said. "Because as of an hour ago, there are a lot of very nervous people downtown who'd love nothing more than to hang this around your neck and call it a day."

He hung up.

Camille stayed where she was for a moment, leaning back against the cool paneled wall, phone still in her hand.

Three names. Three deaths. Three little notes in a file box now marked *paid in full.*

Except hers.

When she returned to the drawing room, the mood had shifted again. People had retreated into smaller conversations, clumps of two or three. Lines were being drawn, alliances negotiated.

Delphine waylaid her at the doorway.

"Detective Broussard?" Delphine asked.

"He's coming out later," Camille said. "Expect police *and* press."

Delphine's jaw tightened. "Wonderful."

"Look," Camille said. "If you have information about the practitioner your father employed—"

"Claude employed many people," Delphine snapped. "Some of them legal. Some of them less so. If you're asking whether he used magic, I have no idea. That was Mother's domain."

"Mine?" Adeline's voice came from behind them. She'd approached silently, like she always did. "Do tell, Delphine. I'd love to hear how you assign responsibility for your father's sins."

Delphine blanched. "I just meant—"

"I know what you meant." Adeline turned to Camille. "If you're going to accuse my family of conspiring with witches, at least have the courtesy to do it to my face."

"I'm not accusing," Camille said. "I'm asking. Did you know about Émiline Baptiste?"

Adeline's eyes flickered. "Who?"

"A practitioner. Related to Mireille. Your late husband kept records of her...corrective work. Devereux. Hollis. Others. Did you approve those arrangements?"

"If Claude did business with someone," Adeline said, "he did so in his capacity as head of this household. He did not consult me on every transaction."

"That's not an answer."

"It's the only one you're getting." Adeline's smile was thin. "We all married things we didn't understand, Ms. Durant. Some of us just read the fine print more carefully than others."

Lightning flickered again outside, far off this time.

The house's lights dipped, then steadied.

Camille felt the tension ratchet tighter, the sense that they were all moving toward something inevitable and no one could see clearly enough to stop.

Three deaths. The pattern complete.

Isabelle's voice drifted down the hall. "What happens now?"

"Now?" Mireille said. "Now the house does what it's always done."

"What's that?" Isabelle asked.

"Hosts a reckoning," Mireille replied.

Whatever happened next, she thought, she was out of appeals.

Now came the fallout.

Now came the narrowing.

Chapter 11
Narrowing Suspects

The first time Camille put a jury in a room and closed the door behind them, she'd envied their privacy. The freedom to argue, accuse, and change their minds without anyone watching.

Belle Rive had become a jury room with no such mercy. Everyone watched everyone else.

By early evening, the storm had pulled back to a sulk. Rain misted the windows. The news van at the gate had been joined by a second, then a third; Delphine had given up trying to count the lenses trained on the front drive.

Inside, the pressure had only increased.

"The police will be here soon," Delphine said, standing in front of the drawing room window like she could block the sightlines by sheer will. "When they come in, we present a united front. No speculation, no infighting, no dramatic accusations."

"Interesting," Patricia said. "I didn't realize 'not panicking publicly' was still an option."

"We're not panicking," Delphine said.

"*Everyone* here is panicking," Senator Mouton muttered into his drink.

Camille sat in an armchair near the fireplace, legal pad balanced on her knee. Old habit. When facts got messy, she made lists.

She drew three columns, neat and controlled.

Motive.
Grief. Revenge. Ideology. Self-preservation.

Means.
Access to the current/ Émiline. Willingness to kill.

Opportunity.
Knowledge of her cases. Access to her files. Proximity to Belle Rive's archive.

She started populating her neat grid, filling in what she knew about each of her "esteemed" companions.

Isabelle: furious at her family's sins, at the legal system, at Camille. Talked openly about debts deserving blood. Motive: overflowing. Means: unknown. Opportunity: as Adeline's granddaughter, she could slip almost anywhere in the house.

Vincent: beholden to LeBlanc favors, terrified of exposure. Motive: to keep his own secrets buried. Means: no known occult ties. But opportunity? He'd done business with Kline, had reasons to know other players.

Patricia: tied to Claude-era cases, including the original Devereux that left Sylvie Baptiste dead. Motive: guilt, or fear of that guilt surfacing, or both. Means: she knew Émiline's history, the concept of the current. Opportunity: deep access to LeBlanc business and Camille's firm through referrals.

Delphine: PR genius, control freak, plugged into everyone's scandals. Motive: protect the family brand at any cost. Means: not magical, but exceptionally good at weaponizing narratives. Opportunity: tech access, messaging control, knowledge of whose fall would best save the rest.

Adeline: the spider at the center of the web. Motive: survival of the family empire. Means: long relationship with Mireille's world, at least peripherally. Opportunity: she owned the house with the archive inside it.

Mireille: practitioner, explicitly tied to the current. Motive: balance, not vengeance. Means: yes. Too much. But her ethics cut against these killings—this was too sloppy, too theatrical for her taste.

And then there was Émiline, the invisible presence at the edge of every file in the archive. Motive: old grief and a sharpened sense of justice. Means: obvious. Opportunity: someone in this house had given her the keys.

"They're not on your pad," Mireille said, appearing beside the fireplace like a thought given shape. "The important questions."

Camille didn't look up. "What do you think I'm missing?"

"Two columns the courts never bother with," Mireille said. "Rationalization. Level of self-deception."

"That's not in the statute book," Camille said.

"It should be." Mireille settled on the arm of the chair, looking down at the list. "Who here can tell themselves a story where what's happening is justified? Necessary. Even righteous. And who can do that without losing sleep?"

"Adeline," Camille said.

"Adeline," Mireille agreed. "Patricia, perhaps. Delphine, on a good day. Isabelle, if you call it revolution and don't make her watch the aftermath."

"What about you?" Camille asked.

"I don't tell myself stories," Mireille said. "I tell clients the costs. Then they write their own."

"Who's writing this one?" Camille asked.

"More than one hand on the pen," Mireille said. "But we can still trace the signature."

Raised voices filtered in from the hall. The LeBlanc siblings.

Camille stood. "Let's see who cracks first."

****

They were in the front hall: Antoine pacing, Delphine poised, Céleste a brittle pillar between them.

"You cannot talk to them alone," Delphine was saying. "We go in together or not at all."

"I'm not some idiot candidate caught with his pants down," Antoine snapped. "I know how to handle a microphone."

"You know how to grandstand," Delphine shot back. "Which is not the same as handling anything. One stray phrase and this becomes about your office instead of Camille's clients and our mother's hospitality. Do you want that?"

"Better me than the family business," Antoine said. "If people think this is about politics, it takes heat off Belle Rive."

"You're both missing the point," Céleste said. "This isn't just about optics. They're going to want documents. Access. Explanations."

"They're going to want someone to blame," Isabelle said from the staircase. She sat on the third step up, knees drawn to her chest like a much younger girl. "They always do."

"Isabelle," Adeline said, appearing at the top of the stairs. Her voice cut through all the others like a gavel. "Come down. If you're going to break decorum, at least do it on level ground."

Isabelle rolled her eyes but obeyed.

Adeline descended with unhurried grace, taking in her children as if they were misbehaving associates at a board meeting.

"Enough squabbling," she said. "The police are coming. The press is at the gate. We will treat this as what it is: a crisis to be managed, not a stage for your various martyrdom fantasies."

"Some of us are not worried about martyrdom," Delphine said. "Some of us are worried about subpoenas."

"Subpoenas we can handle," Adeline said. "We have handled worse."

"Have we?" Isabelle asked. "Worse than a serial killer using our guests as a thesis statement on justice?"

"We don't know that's what this is," Antoine said.

"We know exactly what this is," Isabelle shot back. "We just don't want to say it out loud."

"Then allow me," Camille said, stepping into the circle. "This is what happens when people like us treat law as a game and consequences as someone else's problem."

"People like us," Vincent echoed quietly from behind her. "I hate that phrase."

"Then stop being part of the 'us,'" Isabelle said.

"Enough," Adeline repeated. But the word had less weight than before.

The front door rattled as a gust of wind hit it. Everyone flinched, as if the police might simply blow in.

"They'll want the archive," Camille said. "You know that, Adeline. Broussard knows enough to ask."

Adeline's gaze flicked to her. "You seem very eager to assist law enforcement, Ms. Durant. That's new."

"More like I'm very eager *not* to be *your* scapegoat," Camille said. "And that's a desire far older than you think."

Delphine's eyes narrowed. "Scapegoat implies someone is herding you toward the altar. Who exactly do you think that is?"

"Whoever invited me here knowing this was about to happen," Camille said. "Whoever compiled a box with my name on it in your little records room. Whoever fed my case history to a woman who believes killing my clients is balancing the ledger."

Silence fell.

Adeline broke it first.

"You believe I did this," she said. Not a question.

"Perhaps. But at a minimum, I believe you knew enough to stop it," Camille said. "And that you *chose* not to. Which, in my line of work, is almost the same thing."

Adeline's fingers tightened on the head of her cane. "Tread lightly, Ms. Durant."

"Why?" Camille asked. "Afraid I'll say something true?"

"Afraid you'll say something the police can use," Adeline said. "Against all of us."

"That," Mireille said softly, "may be the first honest thing anyone has said all day."

****

Broussard and his team arrived ten minutes later.

The sight of uniforms in the foyer did something to the house's atmosphere—shifting it from secretive to cornered. Law, in its ordinary human form, had finally breached the perimeter.

"Evening," Broussard said, nodding to the assembled. His eyes found Camille, then Mireille, then Adeline. He took in the room like it was an evidence board. It was as though he was mentally connecting them with a thread and labeling theme one by one.

"We appreciate you coming out," Adeline said smoothly. "This must be a terrible strain on your department."

"Occupational hazard," Broussard said. "We'll try not to track too much mud on the carpets."

He introduced his partner, Detective Alana Ruiz, who had sharp eyes and the posture of someone who had no patience for grandeur. She was all business.

"We're going to need to speak to several of you separately," Ruiz said. "Standard procedure."

"Before you start," Broussard said, "there's a specific area of the house I'd like to see. I've heard rumors about an archive."

"You've heard many things, apparently," Adeline said. "Most of them exaggerated."

"Maybe," Broussard said. "But when three of the same attorney's clients die in three days, staged like some kind of ritual, I start looking for patterns. And for paper. I'm told this family is fond of both."

"It's a private records room," Adeline said. "Mostly financial. You'd need a warrant."

"I have one," Broussard said, holding up a folded sheet. "Signed an hour ago, after my captain saw the report about James's glove compartment."

The slightest flicker crossed Adeline's face.

"Then by all means," she said. "Let's see if you can make sense of Claude's ghosts."

As Broussard and Ruiz followed a staff member toward the east wing, Camille felt the air change again. The house didn't like outsiders with authority.

It had tolerated guests.

It resented investigators.

"Now what?" Vincent whispered.

"Now we watch who sweats," Mireille said.

She wasn't wrong.

Delphine went very still, calculating angles. Patricia's jaw tightened. Isabelle leaned into the banister as if she needed the support.

Camille realized, with a certain grim clarity, that whatever Broussard found, she would be standing in the middle of it when the dust settled.

For years, she'd thought she knew how to read a room. She'd never had to read one while the room itself read her back.

Chapter 12
Revelation & Choice

They didn't make her wait long.

Twenty minutes later, Broussard reappeared in the drawing room doorway, carrying a single manila folder. Ruiz trailed him with a larger box in her arms, its sides labeled in neat black marker.

DURANT.

"Madame LeBlanc," Broussard said. "Have you ever been accused of over-documentation?"

Adeline's mouth curved. "Claude believed in records. I prefer results."

"Records lead to results," Broussard said. "In my experience."

He set the folder on the coffee table, tapping it with two fingers.

"This," he said, "is impressive work. Someone has been tracking Ms. Durant's career like a sabermetrics fanatic."

Everyone's gaze landed on the name.

"May I?" Camille asked.

Broussard slid the folder toward her.

She opened it.

Her bar photo. Her early clippings. Then the list she'd seen in the archive, now under the incomprehensibly mundane light of police interest.

Cases. Dates. Notations. At the bottom: KLINE, DEVEREAUX, JAMES. And her own name, marked with that infuriating phrase: *balance outstanding.*

"Do you recognize this?" Broussard asked.

"Yes," she said. "Your warrant didn't discover something brand new, Detective. It confirmed what I already stumbled over."

"And didn't report," Ruiz said.

"Would you have believed me," Camille asked, "if I'd told you the LeBlancs have a side archive where they keep notes on every time the universe cheated in their favor?"

"We're very open-minded," Ruiz said. Her expression suggested the opposite.

"I'm sure." Camille retorted. "About as open-minded as to thinking I'm not a suspect in all of this when the reality is that I'm likely to be a victim to it all in the end. And that I've been an unwilling, unknowing participant since the start."

"What concerns me," Broussard said, "is that this file suggests someone has been monitoring not just your cases, Ms. Durant, but the fallout from your wins. Their crimes after the acquittals. The outraged coverage. The victims' families."

"That," Camille said, "would be your job."

"It would," Broussard said. "Which is why it worries me that someone in this house has been doing it in secret. And taking...unorthodox steps to 'correct' the ones they didn't like."

He looked at Adeline.

"Who has access to this room?" he asked. "To these files?"

"Household leadership," Adeline said. "Myself. My children on occasion. Our counsel." She inclined her head toward Patricia. "Our archivist, when he was alive."

"Claude," Broussard said.

"Yes," Adeline said.

"Anyone else?" he asked.

A small muscle jumped in her jaw. "We have had...consultants," she said. "Over the years."

"Magical ones," Mireille added.

Broussard gave her a look. "We'll get to you."

He turned back to Camille. "These notations—'assistance requested,' 'assistance offered'—what do you think they refer to?"

"Magic," she said. Enough trying to dance around the issues. There was no longer time for niceties and appropriate "cultural norms." Time to put it all out on the table and let the chips fall where they may.

"Specifically," Camille began, "a practitioner named Émiline Baptiste and the power she calls the current. It nudges outcomes. Trials. Evidence. Heartbeats. You've seen the nastier end of it this week."

Broussard was quiet for a moment. "You're asking me to write 'witchcraft' in my report."

"I didn't ask you to write anything. I'm expecting you to understand that someone here has been using something that behaves like a very ugly, very literal version of karma," Camille said. "And that they've been using my cases as a template."

Ruiz set the box down beside the coffee table. The label faced outward.

DURANT.

"Who wrote this?" she asked, tapping the side.

"Émiline started it," Mireille said. "Claude encouraged it. Someone else has been maintaining it since he died."

"Someone in this room?" Ruiz said.

The room bristled.

"Do you truly think a member of my family has been out driving around killing people?" Adeline asked. "We've all been here."

"We don't need them to have left the house," Broussard said. "We just need them to have pointed someone else in the right direction. Someone with…what did you call it? A connection to the current."

"Émiline," Camille said. "She's the one who can make hearts stop."

"And you're certain he, or she, is here?" Broussard asked.

"I'm certain they're invested," Mireille said. "And that they know my cousin well enough to show up where the pressure is highest."

"Wonderful," Ruiz murmured. "We can add 'summoning vigilante witches' to tonight's agenda."

"Detective," Camille said. "Even if you never put 'witchcraft' in a report, you need to understand the logic. Whoever is doing this believes they're balancing the scales. They picked Kline, Devereaux, and James because those were the cases where the law failed most spectacularly and publicly. But they had help choosing. Someone curated that list."

"Adeline," Isabelle said suddenly.

Every head turned.

"Isabelle," Antoine hissed.

"She's been doing this our whole lives," Isabelle said, voice shaking. "Deciding who matters, who doesn't, who can be sacrificed for the 'greater good' of the family. Do you think she'd hesitate for one moment to point some pissed-off witch at people she already thought deserved it? If you do, think again. There are enough skeletons and ghosts in the closets in this house to—"

"Enough, child," Adeline said. Her tone was quiet and curt. More dangerous than a shout.

"Why?" Isabelle demanded. "Afraid I'll say it where someone will write it down? Afraid your chickens will come home to roost?" She was defiant and indignant. Isabelle seemed to be reaching a breaking point. A point of no return.

"Ms. LeBlanc," Broussard said. "Did you provide these files to anyone outside your immediate circle?"

Adeline didn't answer immediately. Her eyes were on Isabelle, and what stood out was not anger but something closer to disappointment.

"You've been reading too many manifestos, ma chérie," she said. "Good and evil are not so tidy as your pamphlets make them seem."

"Please answer the question, Ms. LeBlanc. Did you provide these files to anyone outside your immediate circle?" Broussard repeated.

Adeline's gaze shifted.

"No," she said. "I did not hand this box to a killer and say 'have at it.'"

"That is not the same as saying you kept it locked," Mireille said.

"Who else?" Ruiz asked. "If not you, who else had access to these files?"

The obvious answer hung between them.

Patricia's fingers were very still on the arm of her chair.

"Ms. Arceneaux," Ruiz turned her gaze to Patricia. "You've been counsel to this family for how long?"

"Fifteen years," Patricia said.

"In that time, did you ever employ the services of a...practitioner to influence legal outcomes?" Ruiz asked.

"No," Patricia said. "I used motions and precedent. Old-fashioned, traditional tools. I don't believe in magic. I believe in facts."

"Did you ever meet Émiline Baptiste?" Broussard asked.

Patricia's jaw tightened. "She worked as a clerk on one of my cases. Years ago."

"The Devereux murder," Mireille said. "Where Sylvie died."

"Yes," Patricia said.

"And when the man you got acquitted died in a very convenient accident shortly thereafter," Mireille went on, "did you ever wonder if your clerk had anything to do with that rather...convenient outcome?"

"I suspected," Patricia said. "I didn't probe. Sometimes, plausible deniability is the best path to choose."

"You benefited," Mireille said.

"So did Sylvie's family," Patricia snapped. "If we're keeping ledgers."

"Someone kept very detailed ledgers," Broussard said, nodding at the box. "And someone continued that work long after Claude died. Ms. Arceneaux, did you advise anyone on which of Ms. Durant's cases were 'ripe' for correction?"

"No," Patricia said. "If I were going to play God, I'd pick better subjects."

"Like who?" Camille asked before she could stop herself.

Their eyes met. Something flickered in Patricia's—anger, yes, but something like regret too.

"That is not an appropriate question," Patricia said.

"It's the only one that matters," Camille said. "Because whoever is doing this didn't pick James and Kline and Devereaux at random. They picked them because they knew they'd hurt me. And hurt certain people in this house."

A draft moved through the room. The candles on the mantle flickered sideways, their flames leaning in unison. The air thickened.

"Oh," Mireille murmured. "She's here."

"Who?" Ruiz asked sharply.

"The one whose name is on all those files," Mireille said. "The practitioner. The current's favorite janitor."

The temperature seemed to drop ten degrees. A faint smell of smoke threaded the air, undercut by something metallic.

In the far corner of the room, the shadow seemed to deepen.

Then a woman stepped out of it.

She looked ordinary at first glance. Brown skin, dark hair braided and wrapped at the nape of her neck, clothes simple and practical. But the air around her felt distorted, like heat haze on asphalt. Faint, ink-dark lines coiled around her wrists like watermarks.

"Émiline Baptiste," Mireille said. "You're late."

"Traffic," Émiline said. Her voice was low, dry, carrying something like amusement. "And storms. And the small matter of not being invited."

Ruiz's hand twitched toward her belt. "Ma'am, you can't just—"

"I can," Émiline said. "You built this place on my work. The least it can do is open a door."

Her gaze swept the room, landing on each face, assessing.

Camille felt the weight of it like a hand on her chest.

"You," Émiline said. "The overachiever. Camille Durant. I've been following your career."

"I noticed," Camille said. Her throat was dry. "Three of my worst clients are dead."

"They were liabilities," Émiline said. "You know that."

"You killed them," Broussard said.

"I corrected them," Émiline said. "Your system had its chance. It failed. I stepped in."

"You're confessing," Ruiz said, disbelief and a flicker of satisfaction warring in her tone.

"Here?" Émiline gestured to the room. "To you? This isn't where my confessions go, Detective. The current doesn't care about your chain of custody."

146

"Maybe it should," Broussard said.

"It doesn't," Émiline said. "But it does care about balance. And right now, the ledger is...interesting."

She moved toward the coffee table, eyes on the folder.

"You've been busy, cousin," she said to Mireille. "Talking out of school."

"Someone had to," Mireille said. "You've been taking unilateral, unchecked action for years. Even the practitioner needs to be balanced."

"Unilateral?" Émiline laughed softly. "Claude asked. Adeline benefited. Patricia chose which cases to prioritize. I just did the part no one else had the stomach for."

"All of you," Ruiz said slowly, "are saying far too many things I can't even begin to put in a report."

"Then make another kind of record," Mireille said. "One that isn't for the eyes of a court, judge or jury. Make a record in your mind and let your soul understand it."

"Yes," Émiline said. Her gaze returned to Camille. "That's why I'm here. You stand at a crossroads, Ms. Durant. You can continue as you are—pretend this has nothing to do with you, let them hang this all on me, go back to winning cases for men like James. Or..."

"Or?" Camille asked.

"Or you can tell the truth," Émiline said. "About what you've done. What was done for you. Who you helped walk free. Who they hurt afterward. You can put your own soul on the stand. Let the current weigh it."

"You want a confession," Camille said.

"Yes," Émiline said simply. "You owe one."

"To you?" Camille asked.

"To the people your wins harmed," Émiline said. "To the current. To yourself, if you have any appetite for honesty."

"And if she refuses?" Broussard asked.

"Then I keep working," Émiline said. "Not just on her cases. On anyone your system fails. And the next practitioner may not be as disciplined."

"This is discipline?" Ruiz asked.

"You've only seen the loud parts," Émiline said.

Mireille stepped closer to Camille.

"She's not entirely wrong," Mireille said quietly. "You've been using legal doctrine as a shield for a long time. 'Everyone deserves a defense' doesn't even begin to cover many of the things you've done."

"I know," Camille said. The words tasted like ash.

"You have a chance," Mireille went on, "to stand in a space where both systems—law and current—can hear you. An old courtroom. A circle. A ritual designed for revelation, not execution."

"You're proposing a...what?" Broussard said. "Some kind of occult deposition?"

"Something like that," Mireille said. "Witnesses present. Questions asked. Answers given under a different kind of oath."

"You're not seriously considering this," Delphine said to Camille. "You'd be handing them everything. Your career. Your reputation. Your freedom."

"That's the price," Émiline said. "Balance isn't cheap."

"And what do you pay?" Camille asked her. "In this little trial-by-spirit you're staging for me?"

Émiline's mouth quirked. "If I step into the circle, I answer questions too. The current doesn't play favorites. Not even with me."

"She's right," Mireille said. "It will show you what she's been hiding. And what everyone else here has been using her for."

Adeline's fingers tightened on her cane again. "If you drag this family into some...witch's tribunal, you will destroy us."

"I think we've done a decent job of that ourselves," Isabelle said.

Broussard looked between them—the attorneys, the matriarch, the witches, the cop whose world had gotten stranger by the hour.

"This ritual of yours," he said to Mireille. "Will people walk out of it alive?"

"That depends what they admit," Mireille said. "And what they refuse to."

"Not good enough," he said.

"It's the only offer on the table," she replied.

The room held its breath.

For most of her career, Camille had lived by a simple creed: manage the story. Control the narrative. Never put yourself on the stand.

Now the only way out involved doing exactly that—in two courts at once.

She thought of Kline's smug smile, Devereaux's quiet contempt, James's crash footage. The candlelight vigil for the boy in the Saints hoodie. The look on Navarro's face when he'd handed her the James file and said, *How many more, Durant?*

"I'll do it," she heard herself say.

The words were quiet but they rang.

Delphine swore under her breath. Patricia closed her eyes briefly, like a woman watching a colleague decide to take the plea.

"Of course you will," Émiline said. There was no triumph in it. Only inevitability.

"Where?" Broussard asked tightly. "And when?"

"The old parish courthouse," Mireille said. "The one they mothballed when they built the shiny new box downtown. Midnight tonight. Plenty of time for everyone to decide how brave they feel."

"Midnight?" Ruiz repeated. "You expect us to just...sit on this until then?"

"You expect to stop it?" Mireille asked.

Ruiz didn't answer.

Broussard looked at Camille. "If you walk into this thing, I want a statement now," he said. "On paper. In my world. Not just in theirs. In case you don't walk out of this."

"And if I do walk out of this?" Camille asked.

"I want an amended one. Or a new one. Either way, I want this shit documented so I have something to go from. There is no way you're going to use this as a way to get out of your responsibilities in this world," he said.

"What's meant to be, will be." she replied.

Émiline's eyes met hers, and for the first time, Camille saw something besides cold purpose there.

Tiredness.

"Midnight," Émiline said. "Come willing. Or don't. But understand: either way, the ledger will move."

She stepped back toward the corner where she'd appeared. The shadows seemed to fold around her like a closing file.

Then she was gone.

The room exhaled as if released from a chokehold.

"You're not going," Adeline said.

"I am," Camille said.

"You'll drag all of us into it," Delphine said. "Our names. Our deals. Our secrets."

"You're already in it," Camille said. "This just decides whether your version of events, your statement, if you will, is in the record."

Mireille touched Camille's wrist.

"Get some rest," she murmured. "You're going to need a clear head to argue with the dead."

Camille almost laughed.

She'd spent her life arguing with clients and judges who thought they were gods—untouchable, perfect, justified.

Tonight, she would argue with something that didn't care about robes or rules—only universal balance.

The thought should have terrified her.

Instead, it calmed her. Maybe it was the sense of finality. Or perhaps it was because she knew all of the masks and veils would fall away leaving them *all* exposed, evaluated and judged without the facades and charades.

And the report for Detective Broussard? Well, that felt like the first honest brief she'd ever agreed to write. So, she got down to the first version. The "In case I don't make it out of this," version.

It was like writing the last testament of her soul so it was officially "on the record," before it either left this plain or was permanently committed to it...or worse.

Chapter 12.5

Mireille and the Ledger

The rain had settled into a steady curtain by the time Mireille slipped away from the drawing room chaos, up the back stairs to the east wing. Voices trailed her—Adeline's silk-wrapped steel—but she moved quiet as smoke, the house's creaks covering her steps. Belle Rive's lamps flickered through wet panes, casting long shadows in the hall.

The linen closet door stood innocent, panel blending seamless with the wall. Claude had loved doors that pretended they weren't there. Adeline tolerated them as long as they served her purposes. Tonight, they served someone else's.

The archive key was warm in her palm. The lock gave with the same reluctant click as before. Cool, conditioned air brushed her face as Mireille stepped into the archive room and shut the door behind her.

Without Camille, the place felt different. Less like a trap, more like what it had always been: memory, categorized and weaponized. Boxes lined the walls, handwritten labels in Claude's careful script, the newer printed ones standing out like fresh scars. The portable unit hummed. Paper whispered.

On the center table, the DURANT box sat as they'd left it, lid closed neat, though the faint crease in the cardboard betrayed recent handling. No one else had been down here yet; the dust on the far shelves lay undisturbed. For the moment, the archive held its breath.

She moved closer, fingers brushing the tab. The current stirred—faint, a low awareness, the way a sleeping animal twitched when someone walked by its den.

"All right," she murmured. "Let's see how bad this really is."

She eased the top folder aside and took out the page that mattered: the single sheet summarizing Camille's major cases, the one the current had turned into a scorecard.

ASSISTANCE REQUESTED.
ASSISTANCE OFFERED.
NO INTERVENTION.

Checkmarks. Symbols. Notations in Émiline's distinctive hand—angled, precise. Next to some cases, the tiny scales symbol tipped heavily to one side. Next to others, a simple, brutal word:

CLEARED.

At the bottom, three names underlined hard enough to dent the paper.

KLINE, MARCUS — PAID IN FULL.
DEVEREAUX, MARGOT — PAID IN FULL.
JAMES, DARRYL — BALANCE PENDING.

And below those, alone on the line where a client name should have been:

DURANT, CAMILLE — BALANCE OUTSTANDING.

Mireille snorted softly. "Of course it is."

This, she thought, was the part no one outside their world understood. You could pay off individual debts—three dead monsters to answer for three catastrophic acquittals—but the axis they'd been built on, the person who'd turned that kind of winning into a career, carried her own separate account.

The current wasn't sentimental. It didn't care that Camille had been ignorant of the terms. Contracts written in outcomes didn't require signatures.

She flipped back through the pages until she found one of the early entries. HOLLIS, assault. Notation: ASSISTANCE OFFERED. Mistrial avoided. Victim suffered breakdown. Public perception: injustice.

Below it, in smaller script, a later note:

CORRECTION: HEART FAILURE, HOTEL ROOM.
FAMILY COMPENSATED THROUGH INSURANCE.
LEDGER: CLEARED.

Mireille remembered that one. The way Émiline had paced after, sugar burning quick in her veins, talking too fast about necessity and precedent. "He was going to hurt more people," her cousin had insisted. "This way the damage stops."

"You sure?" Mireille had asked.

No one had been sure. But once the current took, it didn't give back.

She slid the Hollis sheet aside and found the older cabinet on the far wall, the one Claude had repurposed when he realized his wife's "consultants" were more valuable than her social calendar. Heavy oak, brass handles, chronological labels like a courthouse morgue.

The drawer marked 1998–2002 still hung a fraction open from Camille's earlier invasion. Mireille tugged it the rest of the way and drew out a thinner file at random.

> *STATE v. LEBLANC, CLAUDE* (BRIBERY INVESTIGATION).
>
> VICTIM: CITY OF NEW ORLEANS (TAXPAYERS).
>
> PRACTITIONER: É. BAPTISTE.
>
> CORRECTION: WITNESS RELOCATED. CASE COLLAPSED. CONSEQUENCES REDIRECTED.
>
> *Consequences redirected.*

Mireille sat on the edge of the table and read the margin note twice. So that was how Émiline had justified that one—take pressure off Claude, let some mid-level functionary take the fall instead. The current had allowed it. It was very good at technical compliance.

The more she turned pages, the clearer the pattern became.

At first, Émiline's handwriting was spare, almost clinical. FACTS. WORKING. RESULT. LEDGER STATUS.

As the years went on, the notes grew denser. More commentary. More anger in the margins. Mention of vigil families. Photos of vigils clipped and stapled in, wax stains on the paper where Émiline had clearly used the files as anchors in later workings.

And threaded through it, beginning about eight years back: Camille's name. Not always as counsel—sometimes just as "associate," "local defense," "consulted." Enough for Claude to notice. Enough for him to tag a page and scrawl, in his own hand,

PROMISING ASSET.

Mireille felt her lip curl.

She could still hear that first conversation with him, in this very room: his voice oily with charm, his fingers tapping a ledger as he talked about "cleaning up messes" the courts had made. It had taken her exactly twelve minutes to decide he was dangerous. It had taken Émiline less time to decide he was useful.

"You always did like tricky math," she said softly, to no one.

There was a sound in the back of the room—the faintest rustle, like someone shifting weight. Mireille didn't startle. The current already had her senses on a hair trigger. She turned her head slowly.

"Come out," she said. "You're heavy-footed when you're anxious."

A shadow detached itself from the deeper dark near the far shelves. Émiline stepped into the spill from the portable unit, looking older than when Mireille had seen her last in person. Not in her face—that was ageless, carved by discipline—but in the way she held her shoulders, slightly forward, as if bracing against a constant invisible wind.

"Mireille," she said. Her voice was the same: low, contained. "You always did know how to find the quiet rooms."

"And you always did know how to fill them with ghosts," Mireille replied. She flicked the Durant sheet with one finger. "This is neat work. Obsessive. Self-incriminating. Very you."

Émiline's gaze dropped to the page. "You brought her here," she said. "Durant. I hadn't planned on her seeing it yet."

"You didn't plan on a lot of things," Mireille said. "Kline's timing. Devereaux's theatrics. James's car. The cops sniffing around. The house losing patience. The current nudging her toward the archive instead of away from it."

Émiline's jaw set. "The pattern needed to complete. You know that."

"Three bodies in as many days?" Mireille asked. "That's not completion. That's showmanship."

Silence stretched. The portable unit hummed. Somewhere in the guts of the house, old pipes sighed.

"I didn't stage the timing," Émiline said finally. "I set the lines. The current chose when to pull them tight."

"That's a comforting story," Mireille said. "Is it one you believe, or one you just like the feel of in your mouth?"

"Don't," Émiline warned. A flicker of current prickled under Mireille's skin in response, like static looking for ground. "You of all people know what it costs to question the math mid-working."

"I of all people," Mireille said, "also know what it cost you the last time you assumed collateral damage was acceptable."

She watched the memory land. It showed in the way Émiline's fingers tightened on the file box, blanching the knuckles. Landry. The brother on I-10. The cut brake line. That night had carved a scar in both of them.

"What are you doing here, cousin?" Émiline asked. "You brought Durant to my ledger. You walked her right to it. You're inviting the law to look at my work. That's not loyalty."

"I never promised loyalty to your methods," Mireille said. "I promised loyalty to balance. There's a difference."

"You think they can manage it better?" Émiline gestured vaguely upward—toward the house, the humans, the law. "Adeline and her brood. Their pet DA. That cop with the tired eyes. Durant, with her sudden conscience."

"I think," Mireille said, "that you stopped asking yourself a question you used to lose sleep over: 'How many more people does this working hurt than it helps?'"

Émiline's mouth tightened. "These three? It's not close. Kline. Devereaux. James. Count their victims. Count the bodies that trail them like chains. Wives, sons, workers, investors. You really want to argue that taking them off the board is an overcorrection?"

"That's not what I'm arguing," Mireille said. "I'm arguing that you designed the board. You and Claude and his little club. You chose which cases to mark. Which to escalate. Which to ignore."

She held up the Durant sheet, letting it dangle between two fingers. Inked names caught the cold light.

"Whose handwriting is 'promising asset'?" she asked.

Émiline looked away. "Claude's."

"And who wrote 'axis' next to Camille's name in the margin?" Mireille pressed.

Émiline didn't answer. She didn't have to. The slant of the letters was already an admission.

"You built this," Mireille said more quietly. "You could have just taken her off your board. Stopped intervening. Let her career flatten. Instead, you wound her tighter and tighter around your math until she was the prettiest fulcrum you'd ever seen."

"Because she understood outcomes," Émiline snapped. "Because she didn't flinch from the ugly cases. Because she could look at a guilty man and still do the work. The current likes clarity. So do I."

"And when she started to crack?" Mireille asked. "When the James file landed on her desk and she saw the straight line? What then?"

Émiline's silence was answer enough.

"You doubled down," Mireille said.

"I completed the progression," Émiline said. "Kline was loose. Devereaux was loose. James was gearing up for another round. You saw the footage. You read the reports. They weren't going to stop."

"I'm not arguing they should've lived," Mireille said. "I'm arguing that you aimed your correction through her head. You wrote DRIVEN BY DURANT in the margin and then acted surprised when the police started circling her name."

"That was leverage," Émiline said.

"For who?" Mireille asked. "For the current? It doesn't need help. For you, to keep her in line? She didn't even know your name."

Émiline looked at the table instead of at her cousin. "She knows it now."

"You made yourself a suspect when you started timing corrections like press releases," Mireille said. She softened the edge in her voice a fraction. "Look at this."

She spread the Durant page flat and tapped the bottom line.

"Balance outstanding," she read. "You knew it applied to her as much as to them."

"It applies to all of us," Émiline said. "You. Me. Adeline. Every judge who took a bribe. Every lawyer who buried evidence. The current has a long memory."

"And yet you wrote her name alone," Mireille said. "No LeBlanc box has that notation. No BAPTISTE, ÉMILINE — BALANCE OUTSTANDING. Just Durant."

"She's the pivot," Émiline said, as if it should be obvious. "The others can be handled through legal channels once this is done. Adeline's frail. Antoine's greedy and sloppy. Delphine's obsessed with optics. They'll collapse under scrutiny. But Camille—she's competent. Charismatic. Dangerous in the way only a talented true believer can be. Take away her illusions and the system has a chance."

"And if you misjudge?" Mireille asked quietly. "If she breaks the wrong way? If she turns into something worse than she is now? You don't get to pretend the current will magically reroute that. We've seen what happens when you ignore variables."

For the first time since she stepped into the room, Émiline looked tired in a way that had nothing to do with age.

"What would you have me do?" she asked. "Stop? Let them all keep operating because the law might someday take an interest?"

"No," Mireille said. "I would have you stop working alone."

She slid the Durant sheet back into the box and closed the lid. The current's hum dimmed, approving the motion like the closing of a file.

"You've been your own check and balance for too long," she went on. "Claude indulged you because you were useful. Adeline tolerated you because you kept her hands clean.

"What, and now you're proposing a committee?" Émiline asked. "A little ethics board for witches?"

"Yes," Mireille said. "Exactly that. You don't get to pull hearts like teeth on your own judgment anymore. Not after Landry. Not after this weekend."

Émiline's laugh was short and humorless. "And you're going to chair it?"

"I'm going to sit on it," Mireille said. "With people who remember what it felt like the first time the current hit something it wasn't supposed to."

She let the weight of that hang between them. The cut brake line. The wrong funeral.

"You can hate it," she added. "You can fight it. But you know as well as I do that if you don't accept oversight, the current will eventually decide you're an imbalance yourself."

Émiline looked up then, really looked, the way she looked at ledgers and outcomes.

For a while, the only sound was the soft shuffle of papers as Émiline absently straightened a stack, muscle memory doing what her mind couldn't yet accept.

"You brought the detective here," Émiline said at last. "You're inviting the law into our ledger. That's new."

"It's necessary," Mireille said. "You've been operating in the dark for decades. The current doesn't object to light. It objected to all the unacknowledged harm. Broussard can't put witchcraft in a report, but he can put names, dates, payments. That's its own kind of working."

"And if they decide to hang all of this on me?" Émiline asked. "Wash their hands and say the witch made us do it?"

"Then we make sure the record shows otherwise," Mireille said. "Adeline's signature. Claude's instructions. Delphine's curating. Patricia's silent endorsements. Durant's wins. Your workings. My complicity."

"Your what?" Émiline's head snapped up.

"I didn't stop you," Mireille said. "When I should have. I took money I knew came from ugly places. I let you convince me that some sacrifices were necessary. The current will have something to say about that when it gets around to tallying my line."

Émiline stared at her for a long moment, then breathed out, slow. "You're serious."

"Unfortunately," Mireille said, "I am."

They stood in the archive like that—two women who had spent their lives telling other people what balance looked like, finally facing the fact that they were part of the equation.

The current gave a small, almost imperceptible pulse—agreement, warning, both.

Émiline closed her eyes briefly. When she opened them, something had shifted. The sharpness remained, but the set of her shoulders had changed. Less defiant. More resigned.

"I'll come to the courthouse," she said. "Midnight. For the ritual. For the record."

"I know," Mireille said.

Émiline's mouth twitched. She crossed to the table, set her hand briefly on the DURANT box, then on one of the older LeBlanc ledgers. For a moment, she bowed her head, listening. The hum was there, threaded through every ink stroke, but it felt different than it had when she first walked in. Less hungry. More expectant.

"We're done here for tonight," she said.

"Are we?" Émiline asked.

"In this room," Mireille said. "The rest of it—" she nodded toward the ceiling, the house, the waiting city beyond "—that's just beginning."

She turned off the portable unit, letting the whine taper to silence, and waited while the archive's unnatural chill began to leach away. When she opened the door, warm, wet night washed in, smelling of rain and river and the faint, sour tang of fear from the main house.

Behind her, in the dark, paper settled. Ink dried. The ledger waited.

Outside, Mireille glanced back once, just long enough to know the current was still paying attention.

"See you in court," Mireille told the room, and closed the door on decades of unspoken arithmetic.

Chapter 13

Scales

The old courthouse had always reminded Camille of a church.

Tonight, it looked more like a mausoleum.

The building sat on the edge of downtown, a block from the river, its Greek Revival facade stained by decades of humidity and exhaust. They'd stopped using it five years ago when the new justice center opened—glass and steel and efficient elevators, a monument to transparency that mostly made it easier for people to ignore what happened inside.

This place had no such illusions. Its stone steps were worn by a century of feet. Its heavy wooden doors still bore the faint outline of a brass plaque long torn away.

"Charming," Delphine muttered as they approached.

"It has...gravitas," Senator Mouton offered weakly.

"Gravitas is for campaign commercials," Delphine said. "This is bad lighting and asbestos."

"Perfect," Mireille said. "The current loves the secrets of forgotten rooms."

They'd come in a small convoy: two LeBlanc SUVs, Broussard's unmarked sedan, a separate car for Camille and Mireille. Ruiz had argued for backup; Broussard had convinced her that too many uniforms would spook the very forces they needed to coax.

"Besides," he'd said, "I don't have a checkbox on the form for 'occult tribunal.' I'd like to keep this off the radio for at least one more night."

Now they stood at the bottom of the courthouse steps like jurors called for an unfamiliar case.

Adeline had not come. Whether that was stubbornness or strategy remained to be seen. She'd sent Antoine and Delphine in her place, flanked by Patricia. Isabelle had insisted on coming; Vincent had surprised everyone by showing up anyway. Céleste, Father Rousseau and Vincent's wife all remained at Belle Rive—almost as though they were an offering should outcome not be advantageous.

"I'm not letting you all walk into some weird midnight meeting without me," Vincent had said. "If nothing else, I want to know who's holding the gun."

"Metaphorically," Ruiz had said. "We hope."

Now, under the jaundiced glow of a streetlamp, they climbed the steps.

Inside, the air was cooler, the kind of inhospitable chill of a building with inadequate heating and too much history. The main hall echoed. Dust motes drifted in the beam of their flashlights.

"This way," Mireille said, leading them down a side corridor. "Courtroom Three."

"How do you know which one?" Ruiz asked.

"It remembers me," Mireille said.

The door to Courtroom Three groaned when she pushed it open. Inside, the faint light from streetlamps outside and the spill from the hallway revealed rows of benches draped in stained dust sheets, walls lined with peeling paint, a judge's bench that still carried the ghost of authority.

In the well of the court, the wood floor was bare.

"Charming," Delphine said again.

Mireille walked to the center of the well, set down the bag she'd brought, and began unpacking.

Old legal papers, their edges browned. A small jar of dark water. A jar of salt. A stick of white chalk. A piece of charcoal. A magnolia leaf, pressed flat. A cast iron bowl. A slim leather case that held Camille's bar card, which Mireille had persuaded her to surrender on the drive over.

"Is that necessary?" Camille asked.

"Yes," Mireille said. "Consent by form, remember? You've been signing with your wins for years. Time to sign with something explicit."

She knelt and began to draw.

The circle wasn't a perfect shape, but it was close—wide enough to hold several people. Around its edge, she laid the legal papers, each one weighted at a corner with a small stone.

"What are those?" Ruiz asked.

"Expired verdicts," Mireille said. "Cases this room knows by heart. They'll help it listen."

She sprinkled salt at the boundary of the circle, then poured the water into the bowl and dipped her fingers into it. She flicked droplets onto the floor.

The air grew heavier, like the moment before a summer storm breaks.

Broussard watched, jaw tight. "You do realize how insane this looks from my side of the world."

"Insane is three of my clients dying in three days with matching ritual staging," Camille said. "This is just...procedure."

"Comforting," he said.

When the circle was complete, Mireille stood and turned to them.

"Rules," she said. "If you step inside, you testify. To the current. To yourselves. To everyone here. You can't lie without cost. You can withhold, but silence also has a price. If you stay outside, you listen and live with whatever you learn. And you never speak of this night or what you learn here."

"Consequences?" Ruiz asked.

"For lies: pain," Mireille said. "For silence: marks. For truth: change. Sometimes worse than pain."

"Very encouraging," Delphine muttered.

"Who goes first?" Camille asked.

"You," Mireille said. "You opened this account."

Camille swallowed. Her bar card gleamed in the circle of light.

"Great," she said. "My favorite position."

She stepped into the circle.

The change was immediate.

Sound dulled at the edges, like cotton had been stuffed into her ears. The air inside the chalk line felt thicker, pressing in on her skin. Her heartbeat sounded too loud.

"State your name," Mireille said.

"Camille Elise Durant," she said.

"And your role in this courtroom," Mireille said.

"I've tried cases here," Camille said. "Defended people here. Won here."

"And lost?" Mireille asked.

"Enough," Camille said. "But the ones that mattered here were the wins."

"Do you believe you are responsible for the harm your clients did after you won their freedom?" Mireille asked.

"Yes," Camille said.

The answer surprised her. But the circle did not tighten. If anything, the air eased a fraction.

"In what way?" Mireille asked.

"I built the arguments that got them out," Camille said. "I took the money. I looked at the evidence, knew they were guilty and did it anyway. I shirked my responsibility by telling myself it was the job and that the system would catch them later if they were dangerous enough."

"And now?" Mireille asked.

"Now some of them are dead," Camille said. "And the system is still broken."

A pressure at her temples eased. The circle liked honesty.

"Do you believe those deaths are justified?" Mireille asked.

Camille thought of Kline, Devereaux, James. Of the bodies they'd left in their wake.

"I believe they were inevitable," she said slowly. "Given the paths those men and women were on. I believe a lot of people thought, 'it should have been them' when my clients' victims died. I'm not sure belief matters. They're still murders."

"The current disagrees," Émiline's voice said from the doorway.

She stepped into the room without ceremony, the shadows from the hall clinging to her like a coat.

"But the current doesn't have to file homicide charges," Broussard said.

"It has other ways to make its displeasure known," Émiline said.

She approached the circle, stopping at the edge.

"Step in," Mireille said.

Émiline's eyes met hers. For a heartbeat, something like sisterly exasperation passed between them.

Then Émiline stepped over the chalk.

The light flickered, though there were none on. The faint city glow outside dimmed, as if clouds had slid over the moon.

"Name," Mireille said.

"Émiline Baptiste," she said.

"Role," Mireille said.

"Practitioner," Émiline said. "Enforcer. Janitor. Take your pick."

"Did you perform the workings that led to the deaths of Marcus Kline, Margot Devereaux, and Darryl James?" Mireille asked.

"Yes," Émiline said. No hesitation.

Camille felt the circle's pressure shift, testing the word. It held.

"Why those three?" Mireille asked.

"They were the worst offenders in Ms. Durant's portfolio," Émiline said. "Guilty on multiple levels. Responsible for cascading harm. Free because of her craft."

"You targeted her, not just them," Mireille said.

"Yes," Émiline said.

"Why?" Camille asked.

"Because you symbolize the problem," Émiline said, turning to her. "Smart, talented, proud of your wins. Detached from accepting the downstream consequences. Your name was all over Claude's notes. He saw himself in you. That sealed it."

"You wanted to punish me," Camille said.

"Yes," Émiline said. "And to send a message. If the system will not hold people like them accountable, then people like *you* should be afraid and made to understand that there will *always* be consequences."

"Who chose those three cases?" Mireille asked. "You alone?"

Émiline hesitated.

The circle's pressure sharpened, like a band tightening around her ribs.

"Careful," Mireille warned. "It doesn't like omitted coauthors."

"Claude started the short list," Émiline said. "Years ago. After he died, someone else...helped refine it."

"Who?" Camille asked.

"Someone who understands optics," Émiline said. "Who knows which names would hurt which people. Who knows how these deaths would play on television."

Delphine made a small, involuntary sound.

The circle's pressure shifted toward her like attention.

"Don't you dare," she whispered.

"Delphine?" Ruiz asked.

"You're very good at your job," Émiline said, not looking away from Camille. "Picking which scandals to bury, which to stage-manage, which to let explode because the blast radius hits your enemies harder than your clients."

"I didn't tell you to kill anyone," Delphine said. Her face had gone bloodless.

The circle did not like that.

Camille watched Delphine flinch as if struck. A faint red mark bloomed along her wrist, shaped like the edge of a file.

"Lies hurt more in here," Mireille said. "Try again."

"I didn't give her a list of targets and say 'go murder them,'" Delphine said through clenched teeth. "I asked questions. Hypotheticals. 'If someone were to correct certain injustices, which ones would send the clearest message? Which ones would take pressure off our family?'"

"And then?" Mireille asked.

"And then I didn't stop her when she answered," Delphine said. "Is that what you want to hear? That I looked at my protected list and my expendables and decided Camille's monsters were useful sacrifices?"

The mark on her wrist darkened, then steadied.

The circle had its admission.

Camille felt something in her chest turn over. "You used my clients as PR assets," she said.

"I used your *losses* as shields," Delphine said. "If the narrative is 'someone is killing Camille Durant's guilty clients,' no one digs deeper to realize the real narrative is 'someone is killing people tied to the LeBlanc family business.' It gave us a buffer."

"You piggybacked on Émiline's justice crusade," Mireille said. "Turned it into a brand-management tool."

"Everyone in this room has used her," Delphine spat. "Claude. Adeline. Patricia. Even you, Mireille, when you wanted a nudge for a family your conscience approved of."

Mireille's jaw tightened. The circle's pressure pressed against her, testing.

"Yes," she said. "I've made deals too. The difference is I told people the price."

"And I'm telling her now," Émiline said, nodding at Camille. "Full disclosure. If she walks out of here pretending this is all me, you all get to keep your stories. If she tells the truth, the stories crack."

"Tell the truth where?" Broussard asked. "Here or in my office?"

"Both," Mireille said. "This room first. Then yours."

The circle pulsed. The current liked that answer.

"Camille," Mireille said. "Do you consent to this working? To having your complicity weighed alongside theirs?"

Consent by form.

Her bar card on the floor. The chalk. The eyes.

"Yes," she said, without hesitation. If she went down, they all would. The truth of their pasts would be intertwined—not that they weren't already. But now they would be *bound*.

The word landed like a signature.

The floor seemed to tilt.

For a moment, she wasn't in the old courtroom. She was in every courtroom she'd ever stood in—faces blurring, judges' voices echoing, verdicts read. Kline's acquittal. James's plea. Devereaux walking free.

Behind them, ghost images: the boy in the hoodie. The dead workers. The defrauded clients. The mothers. The vigils.

"You knew," a voice—not Émiline's, not Mireille's—said. It was everywhere and nowhere, a low vibration in her bones.

"Yes," she whispered.

"You rationalized," it said.

"Yes."

"You believed you were necessary," it said.

"Yes."

"You believed you were untouchable," it said.

Her throat closed.

"No," she said. "But I desperately hoped I was."

The pressure in the circle shifted, moving away from her and toward the others—toward Delphine, who had started this cascade to protect her family; toward Patricia, whose silence had long been her currency; toward Émiline, who had taken grief and turned it into a scalpel.

The working was no longer just about three dead people or the cascading rivers of devastation each had left behind.

It was about a system in which everyone in this room had stopped asking where their victories sent the bodies—what blood price had been paid for the sake of winning.

Outside, a distant rumble of thunder rolled over the river.

Inside, in the thin circle of chalk and old paper, Camille understood that whatever verdict came next would not be written on a docket.

It would be inscribed on all of them with an invisible, yet permanent marker.

Chapter 14
The Morning After

Camille woke to pain.

Not sharp—nothing as clean as a knife or a blow. This was the dull, pervasive ache of muscles that had been held too tightly for too long, of a body that had been used as a conduit for something it wasn't built to channel. Her temples throbbed in time with her pulse.

The room was gray with predawn light. Outside, the rain had finally stopped, leaving only the steady drip of water from the eaves and the occasional complaint of a bird testing the air.

She sat up slowly, testing the integrity of her spine, her balance. The marks were there—she could feel them even before she looked. Thin lines along her forearms, dark as ink, tracing patterns she didn't have words for. Scales. Gavels. Something that might have been a noose or might have been a knot, depending on how the light caught it.

They didn't hurt. They simply *were*, like scars from a surgery she'd agreed to while fully conscious.

She stood, crossed to the mirror above the vanity, and looked at herself properly for the first time since the counter-ritual.

Her face was the same. Same cheekbones, same controlled expression, same eyes that had learned early how to reveal nothing. But there was something different in the way she held herself—a weight, or an absence of weight. She wasn't sure which.

The current had taken what it was owed. She'd spoken the names, the cases, the choices. She'd acknowledged what she'd done and what she'd enabled. And the scales, somewhere in the metaphysical architecture of the world, had shifted fractionally closer to balance.

But the cost wasn't finished extracting itself.

She dressed carefully—tailored gray slacks, a silk blouse the color of bone—and went downstairs.

The house felt different. The oppressive weight that had pressed against her since she'd arrived had lifted, but what replaced it wasn't peace. It was watchfulness. The floorboards creaked under her feet like someone taking notes. The portraits in the hallway seemed to track her progress with painted eyes that had always been there but were only now paying attention.

The house remembers, Mireille had said. *Every oath ever sworn on it.*

Well. It had a new oath now. Several of them.

She found Mireille in the kitchen, standing at the counter with a cup of coffee and the morning paper spread before her like evidence at trial. She looked up when Camille entered, her gaze going immediately to Camille's marked forearms.

"How do you feel?" Mireille asked.

"I'm not entirely sure," Camille said. "Calm and level, I suppose"

"Balanced." Mireille pushed a second cup toward her. "The marks will fade to most eyes. But people like me will always see them. And the current will always know where to find you."

Camille wrapped her hands around the cup, feeling the heat seep into her palms. "Is that a threat or a promise?"

"Both," Mireille said. "You're bound now, chère. Not to me, not to Émiline, but to the work itself. You can't practice law the way you did before. If you try—if you take a case you know twists justice, if you bury evidence, if you put a guilty predator back on the street—the current will notice."

"And then what?"

"And then it will correct," Mireille said simply. "Not necessarily through death. But through exposure. Through consequences you can't outmaneuver. You've spent years being supernaturally lucky. Now you're supernaturally accountable."

Camille sipped her coffee. It was bitter and strong and exactly what she needed.

"Where's Émiline?" she asked.

"Gone," Mireille said. "She left before dawn. The binding took more from her than from you—she's been working with the current longer, deeper. She'll need time to adjust to the new terms."

"New terms," Camille repeated.

"She's no longer allowed to perform correction rituals without oversight," Mireille said. "The current judged her methods too blunt. Too much collateral grief. From now on, if she wants to balance a scale, she has to petition formally. Present the case. Get approval."

"From who?"

"From me," Mireille said. "And from others like me. People who understand the weight of what we're doing."

Camille thought of Émiline's face during the ritual—the grief, the fury, the bone-deep conviction that she was serving justice.

"She won't like that," Camille said.

"No," Mireille agreed. "But she'll abide by it. The alternative is to lose access to the current entirely. And for her, that would be worse than death."

Footsteps on the stairs. Camille turned to see Detective Broussard descending, looking rumpled and exhausted but alert.

He'd stayed the night, unwilling to leave until he'd taken statements from everyone in the house about their whereabouts and connections to the three dead clients.

"Ms. Durant," he said. "Ms. Baptiste. Good morning."

"Detective," Camille said. "Coffee?"

"God yes." He accepted the cup Mireille poured with visible gratitude. "I've been up since four going through statements. This whole weekend is going to be a nightmare to document."

"I imagine so," Mireille said.

Broussard looked at Camille. "I'm going to need you to come to the station later this week. Formal interview. You're not a suspect, but you're a witness to...a lot of things I'm still trying to make sense of. That I can't even figure out how to *begin* to explain."

"Of course," Camille said.

"And you're going to tell me the truth," Broussard said. It wasn't a question.

Camille met his eyes. The marks on her arms tingled, a reminder of the oath she'd sworn.

"Yes," she said. "I am."

Something in Broussard's expression shifted—surprise, maybe, or recognition.

"Good," he said. "Because I've spent the better part of the last twenty years watching people lie to me, and I'm quite tired of it."

He drained his coffee, set the cup down with a decisive click, and headed back upstairs to continue his interviews.

When he was gone, Mireille turned to Camille.

"That's what it looks like now," she said. "Every conversation, every case, every choice. The truth, or the current notices."

"And if I slip?" Camille asked. "If I make a mistake?"

"Then you pay for it," Mireille said. "Immediately. Visibly. No more getting away with it because you're clever and well-connected and good at cross-examination."

Camille thought about that. About the years she'd spent building a reputation on her ability to win impossible cases. About the pride she'd taken in seeming untouchable.

All of that was over now. "An honest attorney who can't lie. Won't *that* be a first?" She half-laughed to herself.

She set her coffee cup down.

"I need to see Adeline," she said.

"She's in the library," Mireille said. "She's been there since dawn. I think she knows what's coming."

Camille found Adeline LeBlanc exactly where Mireille had said she'd be: seated in a high-backed chair near the fireplace, wrapped in a cashmere shawl despite the humidity, staring into the cold ashes as if reading entrails.

"Ms. Durant," Adeline said without looking up. "Come to deliver the bill?"

Camille closed the library door behind her. "That depends on what you think you owe."

"Everything," Adeline said. The word was flat, matter-of-fact. "Claude built this family on exploitation and I maintained it through strategic amnesia. I hired lawyers like you to make inconvenient truths disappear. I consulted with practitioners when the law proved insufficient. And I told myself it was necessary. That this is simply how power works in Louisiana."

She finally looked up, and her eyes were ancient.

"But the current doesn't care about necessity," Adeline said. "Does it?"

"No," Camille said. "It cares about balance."

"And we're very far from balanced."

Camille sat in the chair opposite her. For a moment, they were just two women who had spent their lives navigating systems built to protect people like them from consequences.

"What happened in that ritual last night?" Adeline asked. "I wasn't there. But I felt it. The whole house felt it."

"Formal acknowledgment," Camille said. "Of complicity. Of harm. Of the debts we've been carrying without admitting they were debts."

"And now?"

"Now those debts have terms," Camille said. "Repayment schedules. Oversight."

"Meaning?"

"Meaning you can't make problems disappear anymore," Camille said. "Not through lawyers, not through fixers, not through magic. If the LeBlanc family wants to survive what's coming—the investigations, the media scrutiny, the lawsuits— you're going to have to do it honestly."

Adeline laughed, a sound like paper tearing. "Honesty. From the LeBlancs. That'll be a first."

"It'll be a necessity," Camille said. "Because if you lie now, if you try to bury one more victim, cover up one more crime—the current will notice. And it will correct."

"Through you?" Adeline asked.

"Through whoever is closest when the bill comes due," Camille said. "I'm bound to report what I know. So is Broussard. So are the others who were in that circle last night. The protection you've relied on for decades is gone."

Adeline closed her eyes. For the first time since Camille had met her, she looked old—not elegant or regal or formidable, just old and tired and cornered.

"What do you suggest I do?" Adeline asked.

"Tell the truth," Camille said. "Starting with Detective Broussard. Tell him about Claude's deals, about the consultants you hired, about the cases that were fixed. Give him names, dates, files. Everything."

"That will destroy this family."

"This family is already destroyed," Camille said. "You're just deciding whether it goes down quietly or takes everyone else with it."

Silence. The drip of water from the eaves. Somewhere in the house, a door closed.

"And you?" Adeline asked. "What happens to you?"

"I lose my reputation," Camille said. "My practice, probably. Certainly my status as the untouchable defense attorney everyone wants. The truth about the magical intervention in my cases will come out. I'll be investigated. Possibly disbarred."

"And you're accepting that?"

"I don't have a choice," Camille said. "I agreed to the terms. I spoke the words. The current has me on the record and bound now."

Adeline studied her for a long moment.

"You know," she said, "I invited you here thinking you were like me. Someone who understood how to win at any cost. Someone who could help me manage this situation."

"I was like you," Camille said. "I'm trying very hard not to be anymore."

Adeline smiled faintly. "Good luck with that, dear. People like us don't change. We just get better at hiding."

"Unfortunately, there's nowhere for me to hide now. Not anymore," Camille said. She lifted her sleeves and showed Adeline her markings.

She stood and walked to the door. As she reached for the handle, Adeline's voice stopped her.

"Ms. Durant. One more thing."

Camille turned.

"Thank you," Adeline said. "For not letting me pretend anymore. It's been rather exhausting, all this pretending over the years."

Camille left her there, alone with her ashes and her reckonings.

The house was waking up properly now. She could hear voices upstairs—Delphine coordinating departures, Céleste managing breakfast, the normal machinery of hospitality grinding back to life after three days of suspended horror.

But nothing was normal. Nothing would be normal again.

She found Broussard in the foyer, notebook out, talking to Vincent Thibodeaux. The developer looked like he hadn't slept in days.

"—and I'm telling you, I don't know anything about any workings or rituals," Vincent was saying. "I'm a businessman. I develop properties. That's it."

"But you knew Marcus Kline," Broussard said. "And Margot Devereaux. And you've done business with Darryl James. Three people dead, all connected to you and to Ms. Durant's cases. That's not coincidence."

"It's not murder either!" Vincent's voice cracked. "They died of heart attacks and car accidents. That's not—that's just—"

"Suspicious circumstances," Broussard finished. "Patterns. Symbols. Burned legal documents. And a house full of people who benefit from those deaths not being investigated too closely."

Vincent looked like he wanted to run. But Camille, watching from the stairs, knew he wouldn't. He was too afraid of what running would confirm.

"Detective," Camille said, descending the last few steps. "May I have a word?"

Broussard glanced at Vincent. "We're done for now. Don't leave the parish without checking in first."

Vincent fled.

Broussard turned to Camille, eyebrows raised.

"I want to make that formal statement, I promised you." Camille said. "About my cases. About how I won them. About what I didn't know and what I should have known."

"Now?"

"Now," Camille said. "Before I talk myself out of it."

Broussard studied her face, seeing something there that made him nod.

"All right," he said. "Let's find somewhere private."

They ended up in the archive room, which felt grimly appropriate. Surrounded by decades of LeBlanc secrets, Camille told him the truth.

Not all of it—she couldn't explain the magic in terms that would translate to a police report. But she told him about the improbable wins, the evidence that vanished, the witnesses who forgot. She told him about Claude's files tracking her cases. She told him about Émiline Baptiste and her decades of correction work.

She told him about her own willful blindness.

Broussard took notes in silence, his expression carefully neutral. When she finished, he set his pen down and looked at her.

"This is going to blow back on you," he said. "You understand that? Once I file this, the bar association will investigate. The DA's office will want to reopen cases. Your career is going to be scrutinized from every angle."

"I know," Camille said.

"And you're doing this anyway."

"I don't have a choice," Camille said. "Not anymore. I've made peace with the likelihood that my career as I knew it is probably over."

Broussard picked up his pen again, made a final note, and closed the notebook.

"For what it's worth," he said, "I've been waiting years for someone like you to tell the truth about how this system actually works. I'm glad it's you."

"I'm not," Camille said. "But I'm doing it anyway."

They left the archive together, stepping out into the hallway where sunlight was finally breaking through the clouds, streaming through the tall windows in pale gold bands.

The house was still watching. But maybe, Camille thought, it was watching with something like approval now.

She'd told the truth. She'd named her complicity. She'd accepted the terms.

Now came the hardest part: living with them.

Chapter 15

The Human Fallout

The news broke properly on Monday.

PROMINENT DEFENSE ATTORNEY IMPLICATED IN SUPERNATURAL MANIPULATION OF COURT CASES

DEATHS OF THREE FORMER CLIENTS LINKED TO OCCULT PRACTITIONER

LEBLANC FAMILY ESTATE AT CENTER OF DECADES-LONG CORRUPTION SCHEME

The headlines varied by outlet—some led with Camille, some with the LeBlancs, some with the sheer strangeness of ritual magic entering the legal discourse—but they all told the same story.

The scales were tipping. Publicly.

Camille sat in her office and watched her phone light up with calls she wasn't answering. Reporters. Former clients. Colleagues with urgent questions about whether they were implicated. Her assistant had stopped coming to work after the second day, and Camille didn't blame her.

The bar association had opened an investigation within hours.

The DA's office had announced a task force to review her past cases. And her own firm—the partners who had celebrated her Kline victory less than two weeks ago—had issued a terse statement placing her on "indefinite administrative leave pending resolution of ongoing inquiries."

Translation: You're toxic. Don't come back.

She should have felt devastated. Should have felt angry, betrayed, defensive.

Instead, she felt something closer to relief.

The mask was off. The performance was over. Everyone could finally see what she'd been carrying all along. And she could finally put the weight down.

Her desk was covered with files—cases she was withdrawing from, clients she was referring to other attorneys, motions she was drafting to recuse herself from active matters. It was methodical work, the kind of administrative dismantling that came with any career implosion.

But this one felt different. This one felt like an exorcism.

Her office door opened without warning. Rafael Navarro stood there with two cups of coffee and an expression that was equal parts anger and something that might have been grudging respect.

"You could have called," he said.

"Would you have answered?" Camille asked.

"Probably not," he admitted. He set one of the coffees on her desk and took the chair across from her. "I've been reading the statements you gave to Broussard. And the supplemental files from Belle Rive."

"And?"

"And I don't know whether to applaud you or charge you with obstruction," Rafael said. "You just blew up a dozen of my convictions—cases where you won on what we all thought was luck and skill but was apparently supernatural intervention."

"I didn't know," Camille said. "Not at the time."

"You suspected," Rafael countered. "You had to have suspected. Nobody's that lucky."

He wasn't wrong.

"What are you going to do?" she asked.

"My job," Rafael said. "Review the cases where your wins look most suspicious. Talk to the victims' families. Figure out if there's a way to get justice retroactively for people who deserved it the first time."

He took a sip of his coffee, grimaced at the temperature, and set it down.

"For what it's worth," he said, "I think you did the right thing. Finally."

"That's generous," Camille said.

"It's accurate," Rafael said. "You could have buried this. Could have let the LeBlancs take the fall while you walked away clean. But you didn't. You put yourself on the record. That takes guts."

"Or desperation," Camille said.

"Both can be true." Rafael stood. "I have to go. But Durant? Don't disappear. I'm going to have more questions, and I need you to keep answering them honestly."

"I will," Camille said.

He paused at the door. "The marks on your arms. The ones you've been covering with long sleeves. Are those real?"

Camille pushed her sleeves up, revealing the dark lines tracing across her forearms. Scales. Gavels. The symbols of her binding.

Rafael stared at them for a long moment.

"Jesus," he said quietly. "You really did make a deal with the devil."

"Not the devil," Camille said. "Something older. And more bureaucratic."

He left without another word.

202

Camille pulled her sleeves back down and returned to her files.

By Wednesday, the media frenzy had reached critical mass.

She'd been photographed leaving her office. Photographed entering the bar association's hearing. Photographed walking through the Quarter with her head down and her shoulders tight, trying to pretend the cameras weren't there.

Someone had leaked details from Broussard's investigation—not all of it, but enough. The burned legal documents. The symbols. The names Émiline Baptiste and Mireille Baptiste appearing in LeBlanc family records going back decades.

> LOUISIANA'S OCCULT UNDERBELLY: WHEN MAGIC AND LAW COLLIDE

> VOODOO PRIESTESS HIRED TO "CORRECT" UNJUST VERDICTS

> DEFENSE ATTORNEY'S PACT WITH THE SUPERNATURAL COMES DUE

Some of the coverage was sensational. Some tried for sober legal analysis. All of it was invasive.

Camille stopped reading after the first dozen articles. There was no point. The narrative was set: she was either a villain who'd knowingly used magic to pervert justice, or a tragic figure who'd been manipulated by forces she didn't understand.

Neither version was quite true, but truth had never been the media's strong suit.

Her phone rang. Unknown number. She answered it anyway.

"Camille Durant."

"Ms. Durant. This is Congressman-elect Antoine LeBlanc."

She sat up straighter. Antoine had been conspicuously absent from all public statements since the story broke. His campaign had gone dark. Speculation was swirling about whether he'd withdraw from his race.

"Congressman," Camille said carefully. "What can I do for you?"

"You can stop talking," Antoine said. His voice was controlled but edged with fury. "You've done enough damage. Every time you give a statement, every time you cooperate with the investigation, you drag my family deeper into this mess."

"Your family's involvement is a matter of record," Camille said. "I'm not inventing anything."

"You're choosing what to emphasize," Antoine said. "You could frame this as Émiline's solo crusade. A rogue practitioner with a vendetta. But instead you're implicating my mother, my sister, my entire legacy."

"Because they're implicated," Camille said. "Your father kept files on every working Émiline did. Your mother knew. Your sister used those deaths for PR strategy. I'm not making this up."

"You're destroying us," Antoine said.

"You destroyed yourselves," Camille said. "I'm just finally admitting I helped."

Silence on the line. Then:

"I'm offering you a way out," Antoine said. "A substantial retainer. Ongoing consultation fees. Legal protection when the bar association tries to strip your license. All you have to do is recant certain statements. Clarify that you were under duress during the ritual, that you don't actually know what my father's files meant, that you can't confirm—"

"No," Camille said.

"Excuse me?"

"No," she repeated. "I'm not recanting. I'm not clarifying. I'm not taking your money to lie."

"You're going to regret this," Antoine said.

"Probably," Camille said. "But not as much as I'd regret saying yes."

She hung up.

Her hands were shaking. The marks on her arms burned—not painfully, just noticeably, like the current was paying attention and approving of her choice.

She'd just turned down what might have been her last chance at financial security and legal protection.

And it had felt good.

Her door opened again. This time it was Delphine LeBlanc, dressed in sharp black as though she'd come from a funeral or was heading to one.

"That was my brother on the phone," Delphine said. "I assume he made you an offer."

"He did," Camille said. "I declined."

Delphine closed the door behind her and sat without asking. She looked exhausted—not physically, but in the deeper way of someone whose entire infrastructure was collapsing.

"Good," Delphine said. "He's an idiot. You can't buy your way out of a magical binding. The current doesn't accept cash."

"You sound like you know from experience," Camille said.

"I've been around magic my entire life," Delphine said. "My father consulted Émiline for decades. My mother still keeps Mireille on retainer. I've seen what happens when people try to cheat the bill."

"Then why are you here?"

"To apologize," Delphine said.

Camille blinked. That was not what she'd expected.

"I used you," Delphine continued. "I saw your wins, your improbable luck, and I thought: here's someone I can point in useful directions. Someone who'll win the cases that help us, lose the ones that don't. I helped curate Émiline's target list because I wanted your monsters to die instead of ours."

"I know," Camille said.

"And I didn't care what it would cost you," Delphine said. "I saw you as a tool. A very effective, very sharp tool. I didn't think about the fact that you were a person."

She met Camille's eyes.

"I'm sorry," Delphine said. "For using you. For treating your career as collateral damage. For assuming you'd be fine because you'd always been fine."

Camille sat with that for a moment. An apology from a LeBlanc felt like a rare artifact, something that should be preserved in amber.

"What are you going to do?" Camille asked. "About the firm, the family, all of it?"

"Shut down the PR practice," Delphine said. "Cooperate with the investigations. Try to separate my life from my mother's enough that I'm not buried when she goes down."

"You think she'll go down?"

"I think she's already decided to," Delphine said. "Adeline doesn't do losing well. If she can't control the narrative, she'll blow it up herself. Take everyone with her in a blaze of aristocratic spite."

"That sounds exhausting," Camille said.

"It is," Delphine agreed. "Welcome to being a LeBlanc."

She stood, smoothed her skirt, and moved toward the door. Then she paused.

"The marks on your arms," she said. "Are they permanent?"

Camille pushed up her sleeves again, showing the dark lines.

"Mireille says they'll fade to most people's sight," Camille said. "But they'll always be there. Always visible to anyone who knows how to look."

"Good," Delphine said. "We should all have to wear our crimes where people can see them."

She left.

Camille sat alone in her office as the afternoon light shifted and the phone kept ringing with calls she didn't answer.

Outside, the city went about its business. The Quarter hummed with tourists and musicians and people selling Lucky Dogs and promising palm readings. Life, indifferent to scandal, continued.

But for Camille, everything had changed.

She pulled up her email and began drafting a message to her remaining clients, the ones who hadn't already fled:

> *I am writing to formally withdraw from representation in your matter. Recent revelations about irregularities in my past case work have made it impossible for me to continue practicing law in good conscience until these matters are resolved...*

Formal. Bloodless. Honest.

She hit send and watched the message disappear into the void.

One by one, she was dismantling the architecture of her old life.

And when she was done, she would have to figure out how to build a new one.

One that the current would allow her to keep.

Chapter 16
Bargains Refused

The official letter from the bar association arrived on Thursday.

RE: FORMAL INQUIRY INTO PROFESSIONAL CONDUCT – CAMILLE E. DURANT, ESQ.

Camille read it standing in her apartment kitchen, the morning light making the legal letterhead look antiseptic and final.

They were scheduling a hearing. They were reviewing her cases going back seven years. They were considering sanctions ranging from suspension to disbarment.

She set the letter on the counter next to her coffee and found that she felt nothing. Not fear, not anger, not even the defensive spike of indignation she would have expected.

Just a quiet acceptance: *This is what accountability looks like.*

Her phone buzzed. Text from an unknown number:

Meeting. Tonight. 8pm. Mireille's shop. Come alone.

No signature, but she knew the cadence. The formality and bluntness could only be one person.

Émiline.

Camille deleted the text and poured more coffee.

She spent the day sorting through files, responding to subpoenas, and drafting affidavits for the various investigations that were now grinding through her past like a slow-motion car crash.

By evening, she was exhausted. But she was also curious.

Mireille's shop was in a narrow building in the Marigny, sandwiched between a record store and a shuttered art gallery. The sign above the door read *BAPTISTE SPIRITUAL CONSULTATION* in elegant script, and the windows were covered with lace curtains that let light out but didn't let you see in.

Camille knocked.

The door opened immediately, as if someone had been waiting on the other side.

Mireille stood there in dark green silk, her hair wrapped in a gold scarf, her expression unreadable.

"You came," she said.

"I was summoned," Camille said. "By Émiline."

"She's not the one who summoned you," Mireille said, stepping aside. "Come in. Quickly."

Camille entered.

The shop was dimly lit, smelling of incense and old paper and something herbal she couldn't name. Shelves lined the walls, crowded with bottles and bundles of dried plants and small carved figures. In the center of the room was a round table covered with a black cloth, and around it sat three people.

Émiline Baptiste, looking gaunt and tired.

Detective Broussard, looking deeply uncomfortable.

And Adeline LeBlanc, looking like a queen at the scaffold: dignified, terrified, and past the point of begging for mercy.

"What is this?" Camille asked.

"A negotiation," Mireille said, closing the door and locking it. "Or maybe a trial. Depends on how the next hour goes."

She gestured to the empty chair. Camille sat.

"We've had an offer," Émiline said without preamble. "From Adeline. She wants to buy her way out of consequences."

"With what?" Camille asked.

Adeline's voice was brittle but clear. "Money. Influence. Information. I'm prepared to cooperate fully with all investigations—state and federal. I'll name names, provide documents, testify against anyone you want. In exchange, I want immunity for my children and grandchildren. They didn't make the deals I made. They shouldn't pay for my sins."

"That's not how this works," Broussard said. "I can't promise immunity. The DA's office—"

"Can be persuaded," Adeline interrupted. "With the right pressure. The right information. I know where the bodies are buried, Detective. Literally and figuratively. I can hand you two dozen prosecutions. But only if my family is protected."

Broussard looked at Camille. "What do you think?"

"I think," Camille said slowly, "that she's trying to do exactly what Antoine tried to do with me. Buy an outcome. Negotiate a settlement. Make the problem go away with money and leverage."

"Precisely," Émiline said. "Which is why I wanted you here. To remind her that the current doesn't accept cash."

Adeline's hands tightened on the edge of the table. "I'm not trying to bribe the magic, you absurd woman. I'm trying to bribe the *law*. Which has always been for sale in this state."

"Not anymore," Mireille said quietly. "Not with Camille bound. Not with Broussard watching. The old deals are over, Adeline."

"Then what do you want from me?" Adeline's voice cracked. "Public humiliation? Prison? My entire legacy destroyed?"

"Yes," Émiline said flatly. "All of that. You deserve it."

Silence fell and lingered in the air. Harsh. Blunt. Without remorse.

Camille looked at Adeline—this woman who had spent her life wielding power like a scalpel, who had hired practitioners and lawyers and fixers to make reality conform to her preferences. Who was now sitting at a table with the very people she'd tried to control, realizing that control had finally slipped from her fingers.

"There's another option," Camille said.

Everyone turned to her.

"You cooperate fully," Camille said. "Not for immunity, but because it's the right thing to do. You hand over every file, every name, every detail of every corrupt deal Claude made and you maintained. You testify honestly. You let the chips fall where they may."

"And in exchange?" Adeline asked.

"In exchange," Camille said, "the current might—*might*—judge that you've paid your debt. That you've balanced the scales enough that what's coming for you is legal consequence, not supernatural correction."

"I could go to prison," Adeline said.

"Yes," Camille said. "You could."

"I could lose Belle Rive. The family business. Everything."

"Yes," Camille said. "You could."

Adeline stared at her. Then, slowly, she looked at Mireille.

"Is she right?" Adeline asked. "Would the current accept that?"

Mireille tilted her head, listening to something the rest of them couldn't hear.

"The current," she said finally, "would prefer honesty to manipulation. Always. If you cooperate fully—and I mean *fully*, Adeline, no holding back the most damaging pieces—then yes. It will judge you've begun to pay your debt."

"Begun," Adeline repeated.

"You've been cheating the scales for forty years," Émiline said. "You're not going to settle that with one good deed."

With a long sigh, Adeline closed her eyes. For a long moment, the only sound was the distant music from the street outside— someone playing trumpet, slow and mournful.

Then she opened her eyes and looked at Broussard.

"I'll do it," she said. "Full cooperation. No immunity. No protection for anyone, including me."

Broussard pulled out his notebook. "I'll need that in writing."

"You'll have it," Adeline said. "Along with the keys to every file cabinet and safe deposit box I own."

She slowly stood, suddenly looking a decade older.

"I assume," she said to Mireille, "that this is where I'm supposed to feel relief. Catharsis. The weight of guilt lifting."

"Do you?" Mireille asked.

"No," Adeline said. "I feel tired. And angry. And terrified. But I suppose that's appropriate."

She looked at Camille.

"You were right," Adeline said. "At Belle Rive. When I said people like us don't change, we just get better at hiding. You were right that there really is nowhere to hide anymore. And while I don't know if I can change, I'm certainly going to try to stop hiding."

"That's a start," Camille said.

Adeline left with Broussard, the two of them disappearing into the New Orleans night—one to give a statement, the other to take it.

When they were gone, Camille turned to Émiline.

"You didn't want her to take the deal," Camille said.

"No," Émiline admitted. "I wanted her to suffer more. To lose more. To feel what her victims felt."

"But?" Mireille prompted.

"But the current was satisfied," Émiline said bitterly. "It wants balance, not vengeance. She's cooperating. She's exposing herself. That's enough for the metaphysical books, even if it's not enough for me."

"It's never enough," Camille said softly. "No amount of justice brings the dead back. No amount of punishment undoes the harm."

"Then what's the point?" Émiline asked.

"Stopping the next harm," Camille said. "Making it harder, less appealing, for the next Adeline to do what she did. That's all we can do."

Émiline stood abruptly, her chair scraping against the floor.

"I need air," she said, and left through the back door.

Camille and Mireille sat alone in the shop, surrounded by candles and shadows.

"She's struggling," Mireille said. "The new terms. The oversight. Being told her methods were wrong."

"Are they wrong?" Camille asked.

"They're effective," Mireille said. "But they cause collateral damage. The families of the people she corrected—Kline's wife, James's children—they're grieving too. Émiline never factored that into her calculations."

"And now she has to," Camille said.

"Yes," Mireille said. "Just like you have to factor in every consequence of your wins and losses from now on. Neither of you gets to pretend anymore. Or make decisions in silos."

Camille looked down at her marked arms.

"I turned down Antoine's offer," she said. "Money, protection, all of it. To stay silent."

"I know," Mireille said. "The current noticed. It approved."

"It approved of me losing my career?"

"It approved of you choosing integrity over survival," Mireille said. "That's rare. Especially among lawyers."

Camille laughed, a bitter sound. "I'm not sure integrity is worth being disbarred."

"It's worth being able to live with yourself," Mireille said. "Which is more than most people in your position can say."

She leaned forward, her dark eyes catching the candlelight.

"You're going to be offered more deals," Mireille said. "More bargains. People who want you to walk back your statements, people who want to use your notoriety, people who want to hire you specifically *because* you're bound to the current now. They'll think it makes you more valuable."

"And?" Camille asked.

"And you have to refuse every single one that compromises the binding," Mireille said. "Because if you accept—if you use your connection to the current for profit or power—it will notice. And it will extract a cost that makes everything you've already lost look minor."

"So I'm unemployable," Camille said.

"You're *differently* employable," Mireille said. "People who want *actual* justice, who want the truth even when it hurts—they'll come to you. The work will find you. But it won't look like what you had before."

Camille thought about her office, her cases, her reputation. All of it gone or going.

"Good," she said.

Mireille smiled. "You're learning."

They sat in comfortable silence as the candles burned lower.

Outside, the city continued its ancient work: making music, making love, making deals in back rooms and on street corners. The current flowed through all of it, invisible to most, weighing and balancing and keeping its meticulous accounts.

And Camille Durant—once untouchable, once invincible—sat in a witch's shop with marks on her arms and truth on her tongue and something that might, eventually, turn into peace.

"What happens next?" she asked.

"You keep showing up," Mireille said. "To the hearings, the depositions, the trials. You tell the truth even when it costs you. You build a new practice or you don't, but either way, you live honestly."

"That's it?"

"That's everything," Mireille said. "The current doesn't want perfection. It wants accountability. You give it that, you'll be fine."

Camille stood. "I should go. Long day tomorrow."

"More depositions?"

"Bar association hearing," Camille said. "They're deciding whether to suspend me pending the investigation's outcome."

"How do you think it'll go?" Mireille asked.

"Honestly?" Camille said. "I think they'll suspend me. I think I'll probably be disbarred within the year. And I think that's exactly what should happen."

"Good answer," Mireille said.

She walked Camille to the door, unlocked it, and let the night air in.

"One more thing," Mireille said. "The work I mentioned—the cases that will find you. When they start coming, you can call me. I can help you navigate which ones are genuine and which ones are traps."

"Thank you," Camille said.

"We're in this together now," Mireille said. "You, me, Émiline, everyone who was in that circle. We're bound by what we swore. That makes us something like family."

"God help us," Camille said.

Mireille laughed. "God doesn't work in Louisiana, chère. We're on our own down here."

Camille walked back to her car through streets that smelled of jasmine and garbage and the river. The Quarter was alive around her—drunk tourists and jazz musicians and fortune tellers and people selling salvation in ten different languages.

She'd lost everything.

And somehow, impossibly, she felt lighter than she had in years.

The marks on her arms tingled in the humid air, a reminder of the oath she'd sworn and the price she'd agreed to pay.

But they also felt like protection. Like armor.

Like proof that she'd finally chosen truth over winning.

And that, she thought as she unlocked her car and drove home through the glittering night, might be the only real victory she'd ever have.

Chapter 17
Émiline's Price

The courthouse basement smelled like old paper and regret.

Camille found Émiline Baptiste there three days after the meeting at Mireille's shop, in a records room that had been locked to the public since before Camille passed the Bar. The door had been propped open with a brick, and inside, fluorescent lights hummed over metal shelves crowded with case files that would never be digitized, appeals that would never be heard, verdicts that had already done their damage.

Émiline sat at a scarred wooden table surrounded by folders, her dark hands sorting through documents with methodical precision. She wore the same black cardigan Camille remembered from Belle Rive, buttoned all the way up despite the basement's warmth. Her hair was pulled back in a bun that looked like it had been arranged weeks ago and simply maintained, the way some people maintain altars.

She looked up when Camille entered, unsurprised.

"Mireille said you'd come," Émiline said. "Eventually."

"She was right." Camille closed the door behind her, testing its weight. Solid. No one would hear them down here. "What are you doing down here?"

"My work." Émiline gestured at the files spread before her. "Recording. Witnessing. Making sure the current remembers what was done in these rooms."

Camille moved closer, scanning the folder tabs. Names she half-recognized. Cases decades old. Some she'd read about in law school; others were just echoes, footnotes in larger stories about justice delayed or denied.

"These aren't Belle Rive files," Camille said.

"No," Émiline agreed. "These belong to the city. To the state. To everyone who thought they could use the law to hide what they'd done." She opened one folder, showing Camille a verdict sheet from 1987, the ink faded but legible. "Acquitted on all counts. Three witnesses recanted at trial. None of them could explain why."

"You did workings on these cases?" Camille asked.

"Some." Émiline closed the folder with care, like tucking in a child. "Not all. But I tracked them. The ones where the scales were tipped by hands that should have been empty."

She looked up, and Camille saw the exhaustion there—not physical, but deeper. The kind that came from carrying other people's debts for too long.

"Why?" Camille asked. "Why did you help me win those cases?"

Émiline was quiet for a moment. Then she stood, moving to the shelves, running her fingers along the spines of folders like reading braille.

"I was fifteen when I understood what the current was," she said. "My grandmother taught me. Showed me how to listen, how to offer, how to ask for what was owed. She told me it was a gift. A way to serve justice when the courts failed."

"And you believed her," Camille said.

"I did." Émiline pulled a folder from the shelf, held it without opening it. "The first working I did on my own, I was seventeen. A man had beaten his wife nearly to death, and the judge dismissed the charges on a technicality. I was so angry. I went to the old courthouse—the one they tore down in '92—and I made an offering. I asked the current to correct what had been left undone."

"What happened?" Camille asked.

"He had an accident," Émiline said. "Three days later. His truck went off the road. They said he was drunk, but I knew. I'd tipped the scale." She set the folder back on the shelf. "I felt powerful. Righteous. Like I'd done something the system couldn't."

Camille thought of the three deaths—Kline, Devereaux, James. The burned documents, the symbols in ash. The families grieving in ways they couldn't articulate because the deaths looked natural, accidental, deserved.

"But it wasn't justice," Camille said.

"No," Émiline said. "It was vengeance. Vengeance in a nice dress. And the current didn't care about why I wanted the scales balanced, so long as I paid the price for the working."

She turned to face Camille fully.

"For thirty years, I did workings," Émiline said. "Helped tip scales. Made evidence disappear when it served someone I thought deserved protecting. Made witnesses forgetful when their testimony would have freed a monster. I told myself I was correcting the law's failures. Balancing what judges and juries, what *humans*, got wrong."

"And the LeBlancs paid you for it," Camille said.

"Claude did." Émiline's mouth twisted. "He found me through someone else—another practitioner who'd grown too old to work. He understood what I could do, and he was willing to pay well. Very well. Mireille was even able to go to college thanks to LeBlanc money. Bought my house. Built a life."

"And in exchange, you fixed his problems," Camille said.

"In exchange, I convinced myself I was serving a higher purpose," Émiline said. "Claude would bring me cases—legal problems that needed supernatural solutions. Witnesses who needed to forget. Evidence that needed to vanish. Verdicts that needed nudging. And I did it. I told myself: these people are guilty anyway. The law failed. I'm just correcting mistakes."

Camille felt something cold settle in her chest. "When did I become one of those mistakes?"

Émiline moved back to the table, sat heavily. "Eight years ago. Claude mentioned you in passing—this brilliant young defense attorney, daughter of old Creole money, hungry and uncompromising. He said you had potential but needed...refinement. He asked if I could help."

"Help," Camille repeated flatly.

"At first, I said no," Émiline said. "I'd stopped doing favors for Claude after the Hollis case—you remember that one? The securities fraud, the pension fund collapse. I'd helped bury evidence and three retirees died of stress-related complications within the year. I told Claude I was done."

"But you weren't," Camille said.

"No." Émiline's hands clenched on the table. "Because six months later, you showed up at the DA's office with a DUI case everyone said was hopeless. Darryl James. Rich, connected, clearly guilty. And you looked so certain you could win. So confident."

Camille's throat tightened. "You watched the trial?"

"I read about it," Émiline said. "Saw your name in the paper. And I thought: here's someone who believes in the law the way I used to believe in the current. Someone who thinks procedure can substitute for justice. Someone who's going to learn the hard way that it can't."

"So you decided to teach me," Camille said.

"No, I decided to help you," Émiline said. "At least, that's what I told myself. I performed workings—small ones, at first. Made a witness hesitate, made a piece of evidence look questionable. You won the James case on what you thought was skill and luck. And you were so pleased with yourself."

The cold in Camille's chest spread. "And then?"

"And then James Industries killed four people," Émiline said. "The chemical leak. I saw it on the news and I knew—I knew—I'd made a terrible mistake. I'd helped free someone who went on to cause more harm. The current showed me the cost: insomnia, nightmares, the marks on my hands." She held them up, and Camille saw the faint lines, like ink stains, crossing her palms. "I tried to stop. Tried to refuse when you took the Kline case. But you were so good at winning. And I thought..."
230

She trailed off.

"You thought what?" Camille asked.

"I thought if I helped you win enough," Émiline said, "maybe the current would forgive the ones I'd helped you lose. Maybe the balance would shift back. Maybe I could correct my correction."

"That's not how it works," Camille said.

"No," Émiline agreed. "It's not. The current doesn't forgive. It compounds. Every working I did for you added to the debt. And when I finally understood that—when I saw the web of consequences spreading from your wins—I knew I had to stop it."

"By killing my clients," Camille said.

Émiline's face didn't change. "By correcting the imbalances I'd created. Kline, Devereaux, James—they should have paid for what they did. The law failed with them, and I'd helped it. So yes. I performed the correction rituals. I called the debts due."

Camille stood abruptly, the chair scraping against concrete. "You murdered them."

"I restored balance," Émiline said. "That's not murder. That's accounting."

"Tell that to Kline's wife. To Devereaux's sister. To James's children."

"I could," Émiline said quietly. "But they wouldn't understand. No one who hasn't worked with the current understands. It's not about individual lives. It's about the system. The scales. The energy balance. The ledger that keeps running whether we acknowledge it or not."

Camille pressed her hands flat on the table, leaning forward. "You think you're a bookkeeper? You're a killer who convinced herself she was a saint."

"And you," Émiline said, meeting her gaze, "are a lawyer who convinced herself she was a hero. We're the same, Camille. We both used power we didn't fully understand to get outcomes we wanted. The only difference is I'm willing to admit what I did."

Silence settled between them, broken only by the hum of fluorescent lights and the distant rumble of pipes in the walls.

Camille thought of the ritual at Belle Rive. The oaths she'd sworn. The marks now on her arms, permanent reminders of the binding she'd accepted.

"Mireille says you're not allowed to do correction rituals anymore," Camille said finally. "Not without oversight."

"That's right," Émiline said. "The current judged my methods too blunt. Too much collateral grief. Now if I want to balance a scale, I have to petition others. Make my case. Get approval from people like Mireille who think they can do it better."

"Can they?" Camille asked.

Émiline smiled faintly. "Ask me in ten years. When Mireille's made her own mistakes and has to live with them the way I'm living with mine."

She stood, gathering the files with careful precision, returning them to their proper places on the shelves.

"You asked why I came down here," Émiline said. "This is why. I'm bound to witness now. To record. To make sure the current remembers every case, every verdict, every moment someone chose expediency over justice. I can't correct them anymore. But I *can* make sure they're not forgotten."

"That's your punishment?" Camille questioned. "Eternal record-keeping?"

"It's my penance," Émiline corrected. "And my protection. As long as I do this work—as long as I serve the current honestly—it won't come for me the way it came for your clients."

She turned, her dark eyes finding Camille's.

"You're bound too now," Émiline said. "You know that, yes? The marks on your arms aren't just scars. They're a contract. You agreed to serve truth over winning. If you break that agreement—if you use your skills to pervert justice again—the current will notice. And it will correct."

"I know," Camille said.

"Do you really?" Émiline stepped closer. "Because it's easy to make promises in the middle of a ritual, when you're frightened and guilty and desperate to make things right. It's harder to keep them six months later when a rich client offers you a fortune to bury evidence. When a judge makes a mistake and you can exploit it to win."

"I'll keep them," Camille said.

"I hope so," Émiline said. "Because if you don't, you'll end up down here with me. Sorting through the wreckage. Trying to account for all the people you should have helped but hurt instead."

She returned to the table, opened another folder, bent over the yellowed pages.

Camille watched her for a long moment—this woman who'd shaped her career without her knowledge, who'd given her victories and then regretted them, who'd killed to correct her own mistakes and called it justice.

"I'm not like you," Camille said finally.

Émiline didn't look up. "You're *exactly* like me," she spat the words at Camille. "You just don't know it yet."

Camille left her there, alone in the basement with her files and her penance. The door closed with a soft click, sealing Émiline back into her tomb of papers and regrets.

Outside, the courthouse hummed with its usual afternoon activity. People filing petitions, attending hearings, navigating the machinery of law with the faith that it would, eventually, produce something resembling justice.

Camille stood in the hallway, breathing carefully, trying to settle the nausea rising in her throat.

She pulled out her phone and texted Mireille: Talked to your cousin. She's lost.

The response came immediately: She's found. Just not in the place she thought she'd be.

Camille stared at the message, then pocketed her phone and walked out into the late afternoon sun, leaving the courthouse and its buried secrets behind.

But the weight stayed with her.

The knowledge that she'd been a tool. That her skill, her pride, her unshakeable faith in her own competence—all of it had been channeled by someone else's guilt into outcomes that looked like justice but weren't.

And the worst part, the part that made her hands shake as she unlocked her car, was that she'd enjoyed it. The winning. The impossible cases turned victories. The reputation that preceded her like armor.

She'd built her whole life on what Émiline had given her.

And now she had to figure out how to build something else.

Something true. And without the assistance on which she had unknowingly relied.

Chapter 18
Camille's Reckoning

The hearing room was smaller than she'd expected.

Camille had argued in chambers before—motions to suppress, sealed conferences, cases where the public spectacle would have served no one. But this felt different. This felt like being called to the principal's office, except the principal had the power to end her career.

Three members of the Louisiana State Bar Association's disciplinary board sat behind a long table: two men and a woman, all around sixty, all wearing expressions of practiced neutrality. The kind of faces that had seen everything and been disappointed by most of it.

Her lawyer—Maxwell Broussard, no relation to the detective—sat beside her. He'd been her first call after the investigation broke, and he'd taken the case with the weary competence of someone who'd defended plenty of attorneys and won maybe half the time.

"Let them talk first," he'd told her in the hallway outside. "Answer directly. Don't elaborate. Don't try to charm them—they're past that."

"Understood," she'd said.

Now, sitting in the too-small chair with the too-bright lights overhead, she felt the weight of every choice that had led her here.

The woman in the center—Christine Delacroix, Chair of the Disciplinary Committee—opened a folder and read without looking up.

"Ms. Durant. You're here regarding multiple complaints filed against you concerning alleged irregularities in your handling of criminal defense cases spanning seven years. These complaints allege that you knowingly benefited from supernatural intervention in the outcome of trials, that you failed to disclose material information to clients and courts, and that your conduct violated your obligations under the Rules of Professional Conduct."

She looked up. "How do you plead to these allegations?"

Camille's hands were folded on the table in front of her. The marks on her forearms tingled beneath her sleeves, a reminder of the binding she'd accepted.

"I plead responsible," she said. "With explanation."

Maxwell shifted beside her. They'd discussed this. He'd argued for "not responsible," for fighting every charge, for making them prove intent and knowledge.

238

She'd overruled him.

Christine's eyebrow rose fractionally. "Responsible with explanation. Very well. Proceed."

Camille took a slow breath. In her years practicing law, she'd given hundreds of opening statements. She knew how to frame a narrative, how to take bad facts and make them look less damning, how to make a jury want to believe her.

But that's not what she did now.

"Eight years ago," she said, "I took a DUI case everyone said was unwinnable. The defendant was guilty—I knew it, he knew it, everyone knew it. But I believed that everyone deserves a defense, and I believed I was good enough to find a way to win."

She paused. No one interrupted.

"I won that case," she continued. "Through what I thought at the time was skill and luck. Evidence that should have been solid developed chain of custody problems. Witnesses who were certain became uncertain. The pieces fell into place in ways that seemed improbable but not impossible."

"And you took credit for that victory," one of the men said. "Professionally."

"Yes," Camille said. "I did. I built my reputation on it. And when similar things happened in subsequent cases—evidence vanishing, witnesses forgetting, outcomes shifting in my favor at the last moment—I told myself I was just that good."

"But you weren't," Christine said. It wasn't a question.

"No," Camille said. "I was being helped. By a practitioner named Émiline Baptiste, who performed magical workings to tip scales in my favor. She did it without my knowledge or consent for the first few cases. But by the time I began to suspect something was wrong—by the time the pattern became undeniable—I made a choice."

"What choice?" Christine asked.

"I chose not to ask questions," Camille said. "I chose to keep winning. Because asking questions would have meant admitting that my success wasn't entirely mine. That I'd been... assisted. And I couldn't face that."

The room was silent except for the hum of the air conditioning and the scratch of someone taking notes.

"So you knowingly benefited from these workings," the second man said.

"I didn't know with certainty until recently," Camille said. "But I suspected. And I chose not to investigate those suspicions. That's culpable ignorance, and I own it."

Maxwell made a small noise beside her. This was not the script they'd discussed.

240

"Ms. Durant," Christine said, "do you understand that what you're telling us amounts to an admission of multiple ethical violations? Failure to disclose. Lack of candor to the tribunal. Conduct prejudicial to the administration of justice."

"I understand," Camille said. "I'm also telling you that I'm prepared to accept the consequences. I've withdrawn from all active cases. I've provided the DA's office with a full list of cases where I believe magical intervention may have played a role, so they can review them for possible relief. And I'm here, under oath, telling you the truth about what I did and what I failed to do."

"Why now?" the third board member asked. "Why confess this now instead of fighting?"

Camille looked down at her hands. The marks were faint under the sleeves, but she could feel them—a constant low hum against her skin, like a phone set to vibrate.

"Because I'm bound now," she said. "To tell the truth. To serve justice honestly instead of serving clients at any cost. And because three people are dead—former clients whose acquittals I won through supernatural means, who went on to cause more harm, who were then killed in what I now understand were correction rituals performed by the same practitioner who'd helped me free them."

She looked up, meeting Christine's eyes.

"I can't bring them back," Camille said. "I can't undo the harm they caused after I got them acquitted. But I can make sure no other attorney in this state makes the same mistakes I made. I can be a warning. An example. Whatever you need me to be."

Christine leaned back, exchanging glances with the other board members.

"Ms. Durant," she said, "you understand that the likely outcome of this hearing, given your admissions, is disbarment? That you will lose your license to practice law in Louisiana and possibly in other jurisdictions as well?"

"I understand," Camille said.

"And you're proceeding anyway," Christine said. "Without reservation."

"Without reservation," Camille confirmed.

Maxwell tried one more time. "Ms. Durant! I'd like to request a recess to consult with my client—"

"No need," Camille said. "I'm telling them everything."

For the next two hours, she did exactly that.

She told them about the James case, about the improbable breaks that led to his acquittal, about the chemical leak that killed four people two years later. She told them about Margot

Devereaux, about the art fraud case, about the elderly victim who'd died of a heart attack after losing his life savings.

She told them about Marcus Kline. About the double homicide acquittal. About finding out three days later that he was dead under mysterious circumstances.

She told them about Belle Rive, about the revelation of Émiline Baptiste's decades-long involvement with the LeBlanc family, about the archive room full of files documenting magical interventions in legal cases.

She told them about the counter-ritual she'd participated in—the one that had bound her to truth-telling, to supernatural accountability, to a standard higher than the bar association's rules but entirely compatible with them.

And she told them about the choice she'd made: to confess everything, to cooperate with every investigation, to help identify other cases that might need review, even if it meant destroying her own career in the process.

When she finished, the room felt emptied out. Spent.

Christine closed her folder. "Ms. Durant. We'll need time to deliberate. Given the unusual nature of these allegations and your admissions, we'll likely need to consult with ethics counsel and possibly with law enforcement."

"I understand," Camille said.

"In the meantime," Christine continued, "your temporary suspension remains in effect. You are not to represent clients, hold yourself out as an attorney, or practice law in any capacity until this board issues its final decision."

"Yes, ma'am," Camille said.

"You're dismissed."

Maxwell gathered his files and stood. Camille followed him out into the hallway, where the afternoon light slanted through tall windows, turning the marble floors gold.

"That," Maxwell said when they were alone, "was the most thorough self-immolation I've ever witnessed."

"I know," Camille said.

"They're going to disbar you. You understand that? You just handed them everything they need to end your career."

"I know," Camille said again.

"Then why—" He stopped, studying her face. "You wanted this. You wanted them to disbar you."

"No," Camille said. "I wanted to tell the truth. What they do with it is their decision. I can hope that their knowledge that I'm bound to tell the truth, as evidenced by my testimony, will perhaps give them an avenue to *not* disbar me. That they realize that if I'm allowed to continue to practice law, that I'd likely be the most honest representation a client would ever receive. And that I have the potential to become the poster child for what the law practice in Louisiana *should* look like."

Maxwell shook his head. "You're either the bravest client I've ever had or the stupidest, most self-destructive. I haven't decided which."

"Can it be both?" Camille asked.

He almost smiled. "Call me when you get the decision. I'll help you with the appeals process if you want to fight it."

"I won't fight it," Camille said. "But thank you."

He left her standing in the hallway, alone with the gold light and the marble and the knowledge that she'd just taken everything she'd built over ten years and set it on fire.

And the strangest thing—the thing she didn't say to Maxwell, the thing she barely admitted to herself—was that she felt lighter.

The performance was over. The mask was off. Everyone could see exactly what she'd done, and she'd stopped pretending it was anything other than what it was.

Her phone buzzed. A text from Mireille.

> *How'd it go?*

> Camille leaned against the cool marble wall and typed: *I told them everything. They're likely going to disbar me.*

Good.

That's your response? Good?

You're free now. You can rebuild without the weight of all those lies. That's good.

Camille stared at the message. *Free.* She'd never thought of disbarment as freedom before.

Another text came through:

Come to the shop tonight. I want to talk about what comes next.

What comes next?

The work. There's always work for people who tell the truth and don't expect to profit from it.

Camille pocketed her phone and walked out of the courthouse into the thick afternoon heat. The city hummed around her—traffic and music and people going about their lives, unaware that somewhere in a hearing room, a woman had just chosen accountability over survival.

She got in her car but didn't start the engine immediately. Instead, she sat with her hands on the wheel, breathing slowly, testing the shape of her new life.

No cases. No clients. No reputation to protect. No impossible wins to chase.

Just truth. And whatever came with it.

Her phone rang. Unknown number. She answered.

"Ms. Durant? This is Isabelle LeBlanc."

Camille sat up straighter. Antoine's daughter—the young environmental activist who'd been at Belle Rive, furious and idealistic.

"Isabelle. What can I do for you?"

"I need a lawyer," Isabelle said. "Or I thought I did. But then I heard you're not practicing anymore."

"That's right," Camille said. "I'm suspended pending a disciplinary hearing. But I can refer you to someone good—"

"No," Isabelle interrupted. "I don't want a lawyer like you used to be. I want someone like you are now."

Camille blinked. "I don't understand."

"I'm filing suit against my family," Isabelle said. "Against Belle Rive LLC, against the development corporation, against everyone who covered up the environmental damage and bribed officials to look the other way. I need someone who won't try to get me the best deal. I need someone who'll help me tell the truth, even if it's ugly."

Camille's throat tightened. "Isabelle, I can't represent you. I'm suspended. It would be unauthorized practice—"

"Then don't represent me," Isabelle said. "Consult. Advise. Point me to the right documents. Help me understand what I'm looking at. You don't need a law license to do that, do you?"

"No," Camille admitted. "But—"

"My family destroyed people," Isabelle said. "For decades. And everyone just let it happen because the LeBlancs were too powerful, too connected. Well they're not anymore. The current saw to that. And I want to finish what it started. I want to make sure there's a record. A proper accounting. Not the one my grandmother would have written."

Camille thought of Émiline in the courthouse basement, surrounded by files, making sure the current remembered. Making sure nothing was forgotten.

"When do you want to meet?" Camille asked.

"Tomorrow," Isabelle said. "I have boxes of documents from Belle Rive. Things my grandfather kept that my mother tried to destroy after he died. I saved them."

"Bring them," Camille said. "I'll help you figure out what matters."

"Thank you," Isabelle said. "I know you don't owe me anything"

"I owe you," Camille said. "I owe everyone your family hurt. I can't make up for the cases I corrupted, but I can help you with this one."
248

After they hung up, Camille sat in her car for a long time, watching people pass on the sidewalk, feeling the marks on her arms pulse with approval or acknowledgment or maybe just recognition.

She'd told the truth. She'd faced the consequences. She'd given up the thing she'd built her identity around.

And now, impossibly, the work was finding her anyway.

Not the old work. Not the winning at any cost, the clever arguments, the exploitation of technicalities.

The work of bearing witness. Of helping people tell the truth. Of building cases that stood up because they were right, not because they were well-argued.

Her phone buzzed again. This time, a news alert:

> BAR ASSOCIATION ANNOUNCES INVESTIGATION INTO "SUPERNATURAL CORRUPTION" OF LEGAL CASES

The story was breaking wider now. National outlets were picking it up. Legal ethics professors were being interviewed. Someone had used the phrase "occult justice" and the internet was having a field day with it all.

Her name was everywhere. And for once, she didn't care.

She started her car and drove toward Mireille's shop, toward whatever came next, toward a life she couldn't predict and couldn't control.

And for the first time in years, the uncertainty didn't terrify her.

It felt, against all odds, like hope. Like possibility.

Chapter 19
The Verdict

The call came three weeks after the hearing.

Camille was in Mireille's shop when her phone rang, surrounded by boxes of documents Isabelle LeBlanc had pulled from Belle Rive's attic. Papers that smelled like mildew and secrets, detailing decades of environmental violations, bribed inspectors, falsified permits. The kind of evidence that would make prosecutors weep with joy.

She almost didn't answer. The number was blocked, which usually meant reporters or someone from the AG's office with more questions. But something—instinct, the current, simple curiosity—made her swipe to accept.

"Camille Durant."

"Ms. Durant. This is Christine Delacroix from the bar association." A pause. "We've reached a decision regarding your case."

Camille's hand tightened on the phone. Across the shop, Mireille looked up from the ledger she was reviewing, eyes sharp.

"I see," Camille said. "Go ahead."

"The committee has decided not to pursue disbarment." Another pause, this one heavier. "However, there are conditions."

Camille sat down slowly on the wooden stool near Mireille's counter. She was stunned. "And those would be?"

"You'll be placed on supervised probation for three years," Christine said. "You'll submit to quarterly reviews of your case files and client interactions. Any complaint filed against you will trigger an immediate investigation. You'll be required to complete forty hours of ethics continuing education annually, double the normal requirement."

"Understood," Camille said.

"And one more thing." Christine's voice took on a note of something Camille couldn't quite identify. "The committee wants it on record that your binding—the supernatural accountability you described in your testimony—was a significant factor in our decision. We've consulted with... unorthodox sources. They've confirmed that you are, for lack of a better term, incapable of lying in professional contexts without immediate supernatural correction."

Camille felt the marks on her arms warm slightly, as if the current itself was listening.

"You're essentially a living lie detector, Ms. Durant," Christine continued. "Or more accurately, you're bound to truth in ways that make our normal oversight redundant. The committee believes this makes you uniquely qualified to practice law honestly. Perhaps more honestly than anyone we've ever licensed."

"So you're keeping me because I'm magically compelled to follow the rules," Camille said.

"We're keeping you because you've demonstrated genuine accountability and because your binding provides assurance that future violations are effectively impossible," Christine said. "Consider it... a novel approach to attorney regulation."

"I don't know whether to be relieved or insulted," Camille said.

"Both can be true." Christine allowed herself what might have been a smile; Camille could hear it in her voice. "You're reinstated effective immediately. Please, Ms. Durant. Don't make us regret this."

"I won't," Camille said. "I honestly can't," she chuckled a little at just how true that was.

"Precisely. The formal letter will arrive by courier this afternoon. Welcome back to the practice of law. I suspect things are going to look quite a bit different than before."

The line clicked dead.

Camille sat there for a long moment, staring at the phone in her hand and trying to process what had just happened.

"Well?" Mireille asked.

"They didn't disbar me," Camille said slowly, almost questioningly. "They're keeping me *because* of the binding. Because it makes me honest."

Mireille laughed—a real laugh, surprised and delighted. "Oh, now that's just beautiful. The current just forced the bar association to acknowledge magic as a credentialing mechanism."

"Is that what just happened?" Camille asked.

"That's exactly what happened," Mireille said. "You're not just a lawyer anymore, chère. You're a precedent. The first supernaturally verified attorney in Louisiana. Maybe in the country."

Camille looked down at her marked arms. The lines were faint in the afternoon light, but she could feel them—the constant low hum of the binding, the current's attention on her like a weight and a protection both.

"What does that mean for my practice?" she asked.

"It means," Mireille said, "that you can do something no other attorney can. You can tell clients the absolute truth about their chances. You can advise them on what's right instead of what's winnable. You can build a practice on honesty instead of strategy."

"That's not going to make me popular," Camille said.

"You never know. It just may," Mireille agreed. "But more importantly, it's going to make you invaluable to the people who actually want *justice* instead of merely looking for a favorable outcome."

Isabelle appeared from the back room, dust on her hands, carrying another box. "Was that your hearing decision?"

"Yes," Camille said. "I'm reinstated. With conditions, but reinstated."

Isabelle set the box down with a thump and broke into a wide grin. "Good. Because I'm going to need a lawyer who can't be bought, blackmailed, or scared off when we file suit against my family."

"You're serious about that," Camille said. It wasn't a question.

"Deadly serious." Isabelle pulled out a folder, opened it to show pages of chemical analysis reports. "This is what they buried. This is what killed people. And I'm going to make sure everyone knows."

Camille looked at the reports, at Isabelle's determined face, at Mireille watching from behind the counter with her knowing eyes.

This was what came next. Not the impossible wins, not the reputation as the attorney who could work miracles. Just the work. The hard, honest, unglamorous work of helping people tell the truth and facing the consequences together.

"All right," Camille said. "Let's build the case."

They spent the rest of the afternoon sorting documents, creating timelines, identifying witnesses. Isabelle knew her family's business better than anyone—she'd grown up listening to dinner table conversations about which inspectors could be paid off, which regulations could be ignored, which communities were too poor or too powerless to fight back.

Now she was turning all of that knowledge into evidence.

"My father's going to lose his congressional race," Isabelle said at one point, matter-of-fact. "Chances are, this will destroy his political career."

"Are you prepared for that?" Camille asked.

"I'm prepared for him to face consequences," Isabelle said. "That's not the same thing as wanting to hurt him. But it's what needs to happen."

She sounded so much older than her twenty-two years. The current had touched her too, Camille realized. Not with marks or bindings, but with the weight of knowing. The burden of seeing clearly when everyone around you was pretending.

By evening, they had the framework of a complaint. Environmental violations, wrongful death, corporate negligence.
256

It would take months to fully prepare, but the bones were there.

"I'll need to file a motion to be appointed as your counsel," Camille said. "Given my connection to your family through Belle Rive, there might be conflict of interest concerns."

"Can you get around them?" Isabelle asked.

"Honestly?" Camille said. "I'll disclose everything to the court and let them decide. That's how I have do things now. How I *choose* to do things now. Full transparency."

Isabelle nodded. "Good. 'Cause that's exactly what I need. Someone who won't hide things to protect me."

After Isabelle left, Camille and Mireille sat in the shop's back room, drinking chicory coffee and listening to the city sounds drift through the open window.

"You did well today," Mireille said.

"I told the truth and sorted documents," Camille said. "That's not exactly heroic."

"It's exactly what the current wanted from you," Mireille said. "Honest work. No shortcuts, no clever manipulations. Just helping someone build a case based on what actually happened instead of what you can make a jury believe."

"It feels strange," Camille admitted. "I keep waiting for the other shoe to drop. For there to be a catch."

"The catch is that you'll never be rich and famous the way you were headed," Mireille said. "Truth-telling doesn't pay as well as winning at any cost. Your practice will be smaller, your clients less prestigious. You'll lose cases you might have won before because you can no longer use certain tactics."

"But?" Camille prompted.

"But you'll sleep at night," Mireille said. "And the current won't correct you. And you'll build something *real* instead of something that's only impressive on the surface."

Camille thought about that. About the years she'd spent building a reputation on victories that weren't entirely hers, on outcomes that looked like justice until you counted the bodies.

"I can live with that," she said.

"Good," Mireille said. "Because you don't have a choice."

They sat in comfortable silence for a while. Then Camille asked the question that had been nagging at her since the phone call.

"What happens if I make a mistake? If I accidentally mislead a client or miss something important in a case?"

"You already know the answer to that, ma chère. The binding accounts for intent," Mireille said. "Honest mistakes won't trigger correction. It's willful deception, knowing manipulation, choosing to pervert justice for personal gain—those are what the current watches for."

"So I can still be wrong," Camille said. "I just can't be dishonest."

"Exactly," Mireille said. "You're human, not perfect. The current doesn't demand perfection. It demands honesty and integrity."

Camille finished her coffee and stood. "I should go. I have a lot to think about."

"One more thing," Mireille said. "Your first client under the new terms—Isabelle's case—it's going to be very public. Everyone will be watching to see if you've really changed or if this is just a performance."

"Let them watch," Camille said. "I've got nothing to hide anymore."

She drove home through the Quarter as twilight settled over the city. The streets were alive with music and laughter and the eternal hustle of survival. Somewhere in that mix, people were making deals and telling lies and doing what they'd always done.

But Camille Durant was no longer a part of that world.

She was bound now. Marked. Watched by something older than the law and more patient than any court.

And for the first time in her life, that felt like freedom.

Chapter 20
Belle Rive's Reckoning

The grand jury handed down indictments on a Thursday in October.

Camille heard about it the same way everyone else did: breaking news alerts, social media exploding, reporters camping outside the courthouse. By noon, the story had gone national.

LOUISIANA POLITICAL DYNASTY FACES RICO CHARGES

LEBLANC FAMILY INDICTED IN DECADES-LONG CORRUPTION SCHEME

"BELLE RIVE ARCHIVE" EXPOSES ENVIRONMENTAL CRIMES, BRIBERY

Antoine LeBlanc was arrested at his campaign headquarters. Delphine turned herself in at the federal building, her PR firm already issuing carefully worded statements about cooperation and accountability. Adeline, citing her age and health, was allowed to surrender voluntarily to her attorney.

Étienne, in New York, lawyered up and went silent.

Camille watched it unfold from her office—her new office, smaller and quieter than the old one, with a view of a courtyard instead of the river. She'd left her old firm after the reinstatement, unable to stomach the partners who'd celebrated her Kline victory and then abandoned her the moment scandal hit.

Now she had a solo practice. Modest. Honest. Strange.

Her phone rang. Detective Broussard.

"You seeing this?" he asked.

"Hard to miss," Camille said.

"Your name's in the indictment. As a witness, not a defendant. You're going to be called to testify."

"I figured," Camille said. "I gave you everything I knew."

"More than everything," Broussard said. "The archive you helped Isabelle find—that's the backbone of the RICO case. Without those files, we'd have had a tough time proving the pattern."

"Isabelle did the work," Camille said. "I just helped her organize it."

"Don't sell yourself short," Broussard said. "You could have buried those documents. Your old self would have. Instead you handed them over and helped us build a timeline. *That matters.*"

After he hung up, Camille sat for a while, processing. She'd testified against the LeBlancs. Against the family that had hosted her, that had invited her into their home, that had—in their twisted way—tried to recruit her into their world of managed corruption.

The old Camille would have found a way to protect them. To bury the worst evidence, to negotiate immunity deals, to make the problem smaller and more manageable.

The new Camille had simply told the truth and let the chips fall.

Her phone pinged. Message from Mireille:

> *Going to Belle Rive this afternoon. Thought you might want to come.*

Camille stared at the message. She hadn't been back to Belle Rive since the counter-ritual. Hadn't wanted to face the house again, the place where everything had shifted.

But maybe it was time.

She texted back:

> *You know they're going to crucify me, right? But, yes, I'll meet you there.*

The drive north felt different in daylight, without rain, without the weight of dread. The trees were starting to turn, gold and red creeping into the green. The swamp looked less ominous, more like what it was: a living ecosystem doing its ancient work.

Belle Rive appeared around the final curve, white columns catching the afternoon sun. But something had changed. The oppressive weight was gone. The house looked...lighter, and smaller. Still grand, still imposing, but no longer ominous and threatening. Just old, tired and full of secrets it could finally stop keeping.

Mireille's car was already there. Camille parked beside it and climbed the porch steps, feeling the boards creak under her weight in ways that felt honest instead of ominous.

The front door was unlocked. She let herself in.

The foyer was empty. No chandelier glittering overhead—that had been sold, Camille had heard, to pay initial legal fees. No fresh flowers on the hall table. The air smelled of dust and silence. Stripped of it's grandeur and opulence.

"Up here," Mireille called from the second floor.

Camille climbed the stairs, trailing her hand along the banister. At the top, she found Mireille in what had once been Claude LeBlanc's study, now mostly empty except for a large desk and built-in shelves.

"What are you doing here?" Camille asked.

"Closing things," Mireille said. She was burning something in a copper bowl—old papers, from the smell. "The house is being sold. The estate needs to liquidate assets to cover legal fees and potential settlements. But before it changes hands, certain... residues... need to be cleared."

"Magical residues," Camille said.

"Decades of workings," Mireille confirmed. "My cousin performed rituals in this house for forty years. The current is woven into the walls. If new owners move in without clearing it, they'll be dealing with manifestations, strange occurrences, the weight of unpaid debts that don't belong to them."

She added another document to the bowl, watched it catch and curl.

"I'm releasing the bindings," Mireille said. "Letting the current know its work here is done. The LeBlancs are facing justice— legal justice, which is what the current wanted all along. The scales are balanced enough that the house can be just a house again."

Camille moved to the window, looking out over the grounds. The gardens were overgrown now, no groundskeepers to maintain them. Nature was taking back what had been forced into submission.

"What will happen to the family?" she asked.

"Legal consequences," Mireille said. "Adeline will likely die before trial—her health is failing. Antoine's political career is over; he'll probably take a plea deal. Delphine's cooperating in exchange for reduced charges. Étienne might avoid prosecution entirely if he stays in New York and keeps his mouth shut."

"And Belle Rive?"

"Sold to a historical preservation group," Mireille said. "They're planning to turn it into a museum. Educational programming about Louisiana history—the real history, including the enslaved people who built it, the corruption that sustained it, all of it. No more genteel lies about 'heritage.'"

"Good," Camille said.

They worked together for the next hour, burning documents, clearing spaces, speaking words in French and languages older than French that released bindings and settled accounts. Camille didn't understand all of it, but she could feel the house... exhaling. Letting go.

In Claude's old archive room, they found one last cache of files—records of workings that predated Émiline, going back to the 1920s. The LeBlancs had been consulting practitioners for generations.

"It's in the bones of the family," Mireille said, sorting through yellowed pages. "This belief that rules are for other people. That power means the right to cheat."

"Will that end now?" Camille asked. "With the indictments?"

"The family's power will end," Mireille said. "But that belief—that's woven into Louisiana itself. Into every courthouse and backroom deal. The LeBlancs just did it more blatantly than most."

She burned the last of the old records and spoke a final word. The air in the archive room shifted, became lighter.

"There," Mireille said. "Done. The house is clean. Just stone and wood now, no ghosts, no whispering."

They walked through Belle Rive one last time—through the ballroom where Camille had first met the assembled guests, through the dining room where they'd shared tense meals, through the drawing room where Adeline had held court.

In each space, Camille felt the absence of what had been there before. The watching. The listening. The judging. The weight of accumulated sins.

"It's strange," Camille said. "The house almost feels sad and lonely."

"It is," Mireille said. "It's old and ready to rest at last. It's held too many secrets for too long. Being a museum will be far easier."

At the front door, Mireille paused, placed her hand flat against the doorframe, and spoke something too quiet for Camille to hear. A blessing, maybe. Or a farewell.

Outside, the October sun was starting to slant low, turning the white columns gold.

"What about Isabelle?" Camille asked. "Where does she fit in all this?"

"Isabelle's free," Mireille said. "She was never part of the corruption—too young, too idealistic. The current has no claim on her. She gets to build something new."

"With our help," Camille added.

"With your help," Mireille corrected. "I'm just the consultant. You're her attorney."

They stood on the porch for a moment, looking at the house in the fading light.

"It really is just a house now," Camille said.

"Yes," Mireille agreed. "Just a beautiful, sad, empty house with a terrible history and a chance at a better future. Like a lot of things in Louisiana."

As they drove away, Camille looked back once in her rearview mirror. Belle Rive stood there against the darkening sky, white and still and somehow peaceful.

The current had finished its work here. The scales were balanced. Justice—imperfect, incomplete, but real—had been served.

Now came the harder part: making sure it stuck.

Chapter 20.5

Sarah Chen

Three weeks after Belle Rive, Camille's office felt like a cage she'd built herself. The binding thrummed faint under her skin—a constant awareness, like a bruise that didn't hurt until pressed. It hadn't stopped her from working. If anything, it sharpened her edges.

Sarah Chen walked in on a Tuesday, 4:13 p.m., rain drumming the window. Mid-thirties, sharp bob, suit off-the-rack but pressed crisp. Eyes red-rimmed but dry, the kind of controlled grief Camille knew from gallery seats.

"Ms. Durant." Sarah extended a hand, grip firm. "Thank you for seeing me. Referral from the civil rights coalition."

"Call me Camille." She gestured to the client chair. "Coffee?"

Sarah shook her head, settling a slim folder on her lap. "I'll be quick. My husband—former husband—was a Baton Rouge cop. Internal Affairs ruled his death suicide last year. Ruled it clean. I don't believe it."

Camille opened her notepad, pen poised. Binding stirred—subtle prickle, like listening. "Why not?"

"He'd been whistleblowing. Corruption ring in the precinct— kickbacks from tow companies, evidence tampering, planted drugs on stops. Names higher up. They buried him in psych evals, antidepressants in his locker. Ruled it depression."

Evidence rundown followed: coroner report, IA file, texts timestamped. Solid paper trail, motive clear. Camille's old instincts fired—suppression angles, chain gaps, character assassinations.

She leaned forward. "Civil suit? Wrongful death, civil rights violation under 1983?"

"Exactly." Sarah slid photos across: husband's badge, last email (*They're closing in. Protect Riley.*). "Department settled quiet with NDAs. I want public trial. Accountability."

Binding tightened—Camille felt the pull when she pictured the playbook: bury the emails as hearsay, smear psych history, lean on "suicide epidemic" stats. Old Camille would've run it smooth, odds 70/30 defense win.

New terms hummed: Truth, not trick.

"What's your endgame?" Camille asked. "Money? Statement?"

Sarah met her eyes. "His name clean. Others safe. No more Rogers."

Camille nodded, flipping the file. "Strong case on paper, but uphill. IA immunity's thick. Need discovery hits—emails, dash cams, priors on named officers. They'll fight dirty: your divorce records, his evals. Public smears."

"I know." Sarah's voice held steady. "That's why you. Word is you don't fold."

Used to, Camille thought. Binding warmed approval.

"Let's map it." She pulled a fresh sheet. "Liability first: supervisor knowledge. Then punitive damages. Settlement floor?"

Talk flowed two hours—strategy unvarnished, risks plain. No shading. Camille laid the 40% loss odds bare, flagged weak witnesses, sketched counters. Sarah nodded, took notes, asked sharp follow-ups.

At the door, folder under arm: "You're different than I expected."

Camille raised a brow. "How?"

"Reviews said ruthless. You're...honest."

"Life changes the angles," Camille said.

Sarah paused. "Riley starts college next year. Clean name matters."

"We'll get it."

Door clicked shut. Binding eased—no tug, no warning. First case under new rules: straight law, no shortcuts.

Camille stared at the notepad. *Sarah Chen v. BRPD*. Scales even, for once.

Chapter 21
New Terms

Camille stood in Mireille's shop with a problem.

"I have a client," she said. "Or I might have a client. I can't decide if I should take the case."

"Tell me," Mireille said, setting down the bundle of herbs she'd been preparing.

"Woman named Sarah Chen. Her brother was killed by police during a traffic stop. The official report says he reached for something, appeared threatening. But Sarah has dashcam footage that tells a different story. She wants to sue—civil rights violation, wrongful death, the works."

"Sounds straightforward," Mireille said. "Why the hesitation?"

"Because I did some research," Camille said. "The officer involved has a history. Three previous incidents, all ruled justified, all with families who say the reports were lies. But there's never been enough evidence to challenge the official narrative."

"Until now," Mireille said.

"Until now." Camille sat on the wooden stool, pulled out her phone, showed Mireille a photo of the dashcam footage. "This is clear. Unambiguous. Sarah's brother had his hands up. He was complying. The officer shot him anyway."

Mireille studied the image. "So take the case."

"It's going to be ugly," Camille said. "The police union will fight back hard. There'll be pressure—political, personal, maybe dangerous. The easy thing would be to refer her to someone else, someone with more resources, someone who specializes in civil rights work."

"But?" Mireille prompted.

"But she came to me specifically," Camille said. "She'd heard about the LeBlanc case, about my binding, about my... reputation for honesty. She said she needs a lawyer who can't be bought or scared off. Someone the current won't let lie."

Mireille smiled. "And there's the real question. Not whether you can take the case, but whether the current wants you to."

Camille looked down at her arms. The marks were almost invisible now to normal eyes, faded to the point where she could pass as unmarked. But they were there. Always there.

"How do I know?" she asked. "How do I know if this is a case the current wants me to take versus one I should refer out?"

"You ask," Mireille said simply.

She moved to the back of the shop, to a small altar covered with candles and offerings. From a drawer, she pulled out a leather-bound journal—not old, maybe a few years, pages filled with Mireille's neat handwriting.

"This is my working log," Mireille said. "Every petition I make to the current, every question I ask, every answer I receive. It keeps me honest. Accountable."

She opened to a blank page and dated it. Then she looked at Camille.

"You need to start keeping one too," Mireille said. "You're bound now. That means you have access—limited access, but real. You can ask the current for guidance on cases that touch its areas of concern: justice perverted, legal corruption, imbalances that the law can't or won't address."

"I'm not a practitioner," Camille said. "I don't do workings."

"You don't manipulate outcomes," Mireille corrected. "But you can ask for clarity. For confirmation that a case is within your binding's scope. The current will answer—not with words, but with feelings, signs, certainties you can't explain but can't deny."

She lit a candle, the flame casting moving shadows.

"Ask about Sarah Chen's case," Mireille said. "Ask if this is work the current wants from you."

Camille felt foolish for a moment, like she was playacting at something she didn't understand. But then she thought of Sarah Chen's face when she'd told her story—the grief, the anger, the desperate need for someone to care about the truth.

She closed her eyes. Took a breath. And asked, silently: Is this mine to do?

The marks on her arms flared warm. Not painfully—just present, certain, undeniable. And in that warmth came a feeling she couldn't have articulated but understood completely:

Yes. This is yours. This is exactly yours.

She opened her eyes.

"The current says yes," she said.

"I know," Mireille said. "I felt it from here. The shop's protections recognized the answer. You're cleared to take the case."

Camille pulled out her phone and texted Sarah Chen:

> *I'll represent you. Come to my office tomorrow and we'll start building the case.*

The response came immediately:

> *Thank you. Thank you so much.*

After she pocketed her phone, Camille looked at Mireille. "This is going to be my practice now, isn't it? Cases the current approves. Work that balances scales instead of just winning."

"Yes," Mireille said. "You'll still take normal cases—divorces, contracts, whatever pays the bills. But the important work, the cases that matter, those will come to you through the current. People who need honest advocacy. Situations where the truth is being buried and someone needs to dig it up."

"That's not a practice," Camille said. "That's a calling."

"It's both," Mireille said. "And it's what you agreed to when you participated in the counter-ritual. You bound yourself to serve justice honestly. The current is going to hold you to that."

She handed Camille a journal similar to her own—blank pages, leather cover, simple and functional.

"Start keeping records," Mireille said. "Not just case notes, but reflections. What you learned, what you struggled with, how the current guided you. It'll help you understand the work better. And it'll be useful when the current sends you clients who need proof that you're not just another lawyer making promises."

Camille took the journal, felt its weight in her hands.

"What about cases where the current doesn't give me an answer?" she asked. "Where I ask for guidance and get nothing?"

"Then you make the decision yourself," Mireille said. "The current isn't going to micromanage you. It trusts you to use your judgment on routine matters. It only weighs in on cases that touch its specific concerns—corruption, perverted justice, scales that need balancing."

"So I'm still a lawyer," Camille said. "Just one with supernatural oversight on certain matters."

"Exactly," Mireille said. "Think of the current as a specialized supervising attorney. One who can't be fooled and doesn't accept excuses."

Camille laughed despite herself. "That's a terrifying way to practice law."

"It's an honest way to practice law," Mireille said. "Which, in Louisiana, might be more revolutionary than anything else we've done."

They worked together for a while, Mireille teaching Camille the basics of petition and discernment. How to ask questions clearly. How to recognize the current's answers. How to distinguish between her own fears and the current's actual guidance.

"You're not going to be perfect at this," Mireille said. "You'll misread signs, make mistakes, take cases you should have referred. But as long as you're honest about it—as long as you acknowledge errors and try to do better—the current will work with you."

"What if I really screw up?" Camille asked. "What if I take a case and realize halfway through that I'm in over my head?"

"Then you tell your client the truth," Mireille said. "You say: I made a mistake taking this case, here's a better attorney for you, I'm sorry. The current values honesty over competence. It would rather you admit you're wrong than bluff your way through."

"That's going to be hard," Camille said.

"Everything worth doing is hard," Mireille said. "You spent years building a reputation on never admitting weakness. Now you have to build a new reputation on consistently admitting that you are imperfect and have weaknesses. Part of your penance is accepting that you're not infallible. Be honest about your limitations instead of pretending you don't have any."

She blew out the candle, and the shop settled into comfortable dimness.

"There's one more thing," Mireille said. "The current's network extends beyond Louisiana. There are practitioners in other cities, other states, who work with the same forces. Chicago, especially. There's a lineage there, tied to prohibition-era speakeasies and the corruption that built that city."

"Why are you telling me this?" Camille asked.

"Because you might get clients from out of state," Mireille said. "Or you might need to consult with practitioners who understand the current in different contexts. What we do here—this isn't unique to Louisiana. It's just that Louisiana is more honest about its ghosts than most places."

She pulled a business card from a drawer—black, like Camille's had been, but with different symbols. An address in Chicago. A phone number. Nothing else.

"If you ever need to reach someone who understands the work in that city, call this number," Mireille said. "Tell them I sent you. They'll know what it means."

Camille pocketed the card without looking at it too closely. "Should I be worried that you're already planning for me to need out-of-state help?"

"I'm planning for the current to use you in ways we haven't imagined yet," Mireille said. "I didn't see that decision coming – to not disbar you. You're the first attorney in modern practice to be bound this way. That makes you a resource and an anomaly. You're charting new territory, Camille. People will hear about you. They'll come looking for someone who can't lie, can't be corrupted, can't take a case without supernatural approval when it matters."

"I just wanted to be able to keep practicing law," Camille said.

"And now you will," Mireille said. "Just not the way you thought. Welcome to the work, chère. The real work. The kind that lasts."

Camille left the shop as evening settled over the Quarter. The streets were filling with tourists and musicians, people looking for good times and good luck and escapes from whatever waited for them at home.

She walked past them all, journal tucked under her arm, feeling the marks on her skin like a secret language only she and the current understood.

Tomorrow she'd meet with Sarah Chen and start building a case against a corrupt police department. Next week she'd appear in court on Isabelle's environmental suit. Next month, who knew—another case the current sent her way, another opportunity to balance scales and speak truth and do the work that mattered.

It wouldn't make her rich. It wouldn't make her famous. It would probably make her a target for people who preferred their lawyers malleable and their justice negotiable.

But it would be honest. It would be real. And it would be hers.

She pulled out her phone and opened a note titled "Chen case - initial thoughts." Started typing:

> *Client needs advocate who can't be compromised. Case involves clear evidence of wrongdoing being covered by institutional power. Current has confirmed this is within*

binding's scope. Proceed with full transparency about my limitations and my obligations.

She paused, then added:

Remember: truth over winning. Justice over outcomes. Balance over reputation.

The words looked stark on the screen. A mission statement for a practice she was building one honest case at a time.

Camille Durant had spent ten years being the attorney everyone wanted when they needed someone clever and ruthless and willing to bend every rule.

Now she was becoming the attorney people needed when they wanted someone who couldn't lie even if it cost her everything.

The current had made sure of that.

And somehow, impossibly, she was grateful.

Chapter 21.5
Balances Cleared

Camille sat alone in her shotgun house kitchen, the ledger open under a single lamp. Midnight humidity pressed the windows, New Orleans breathing heavy outside. The binding was quiet now—companion hum, not leash.

Pages yellowed under her fingers. Names crossed deliberate: Kline—paid. Devereux—paid. James—paid. Her own line below, Émiline's slant precise:

DURANT, CAMILLE — OUTSTANDING → SETTLED.

No fanfare. No scales tipping audible. Just ink, dry and final.

Sarah's case folder beside it—officers named, IA crumbling. Mireille's words from last week: "Binding tests intent. You passed."

Camille traced the scales symbol, balanced now. Rot reversed. Ledger even.

Outside, bayou wind rattled shutters. Current sighed content, river finding level.

She closed the book.

TERMS MET.

Epilogue
A Different Kind of Case

The rain had finally broken the heat.

Camille stood at her kitchen sink and watched it fall in clean, vertical sheets, turning the street outside into a blurred watercolor. The Quarter sounded different in the rain—muted brass from a distant trumpet, tires hissing on wet asphalt, the occasional shout softened into something almost musical.

Her phone lay face-down on the table behind her. The email had come an hour ago.

> DECISION OF THE LOUISIANA STATE BAR DISCIPLINARY COMMITTEE RE: CAMILLE E. DURANT

She'd read it twice. The language was dense, careful, written by people who understood that they were setting a precedent and were deeply uncomfortable about it.

The suspension lifted.

No disbarment.

Conditions attached.

Periodic ethics reviews. Mandatory disclosure to all potential clients regarding the history of unsolicited supernatural intervention in her cases. An agreement that any future knowledge of magical workings affecting court outcomes had to be reported to both the bar and relevant authorities.

And one line, buried near the end, that had made her laugh out loud:

> *Given Ms. Durant's demonstrated inability, under current metaphysical constraints, to materially misrepresent facts without immediate consequence, the Committee finds that her continued licensure—under strict supervision—may, paradoxically, advance the interests of justice.*

Paradoxically. They'd really used the word.

She turned from the window and picked up the printed decision, feeling the weight of it in her hand. A decade ago, she would have framed it as a win: leverage, proof that she'd out-argued the system again.

Now it felt more like a tool. Heavy, dangerous, but potentially useful.

Her door buzzed.

She checked the monitor. Mireille, hood up against the rain, holding a paper bag in one hand and a folder under the other.

Camille let her in.

"You look like someone who just survived a firing squad," Mireille said, shrugging off her damp jacket. "How'd they phrase it? 'We would very much like to disbar you, but unfortunately you are now too honest to kill.'"

"Close," Camille said. "They're keeping me. On a leash. Supervised, reviewed, subject to more audits than a Fortune 500 company."

Mireille set the bag on the table and pulled out two containers of steaming gumbo. "Congratulations. You're officially a state-approved witch lawyer."

Camille snorted. "Don't say that where they can hear you." She winked.

"They already know." Mireille slid a container toward her. "Eat. You look like you've been living on coffee and regret."

Camille sat, the decision between them like a third plate. "How's Émiline?"

"Stubborn. Exhausted. Somewhat bored being stuck in the bowels of the archives," Mireille opened the folder she'd been carrying, laying out a neat sheaf of photocopies. "Obsessed with her files. She's started building her own archive now—cases the current wants watched. She said to tell you you're in three of them."

"Of course I am," Camille said. "Which ones?"

"The ones where people will try to use you the way Antoine tried to," Mireille said. "The current wants a record of every time you say no."

Camille picked up one of the photocopies. It was from a local paper, yellowed, the text blurred in places.

"Why the ancient clipping?" she asked.

"That one's not about you," Mireille said. "Or about here."

The paper wasn't local, she realized. The masthead at the top read: CHICAGO HERALD, the date below it: October 3, 1925.

Camille's stomach did a small, precise drop—as if an elevator had started to move without warning.

The headline was short and unhelpful:

TRAGIC FIRE IN SOUTH SIDE CLUB; SIX DEAD.

She skimmed the column. A late-night blaze in an unlicensed drinking establishment. Rumors of mob involvement. Police insisting there was "no evidence of foul play," despite witnesses insisting the fire had started in three places at once.

None of that was what made the skin along her arms prickle.

It was the photograph.

290

Grainy, black-and-white, but clear enough. The club's entrance—a narrow door beneath a sign that read LEDA'S—charred around the edges. And on the brick to the right of the door, half-hidden by smoke and soot, was a familiar symbol.

Scales. Crooked. Tilted.

Exactly like the marks on her arms.

She set the page down carefully.

"Where did you get this?" Camille asked.

"Émiline found it in an old box that didn't belong to her," Mireille said. "Someone—before all of us—was clipping stories like this. Fires, accidents, suspicious acquittals followed by convenient deaths. Some in Louisiana. Some in New York. Some in Chicago."

"Leda's," Camille said slowly. "South Side club. Six dead."

"Speakeasy," Mireille said. "Run by a woman with a talent for getting the wrong people off at the right time. According to the whispers."

"The current was there," Camille said. It wasn't a question.

"It's there," Mireille corrected. "The current isn't bound to Louisiana. It likes certain climates, certain architectures—places where the law and human desperation meet. Courthouses.

Casinos. Rivers. Clubs where everyone's breaking the rules and pretending it doesn't cost anything."

Camille traced the blurred scales in the photo with one fingertip.

"Who clipped this?" she asked.

"We don't know," Mireille said. "The box was in the back of an old clerk's office. No name, no note. Just patterns. Someone else was watching before us. Keeping records. Maybe working. Maybe just... noticing."

"Keeping a ledger," Camille said.

Mireille nodded. "The current likes ledgers. You're not the first to cross paths with it, Camille. You just happen to be our century's favorite and the only one the current is using for bigger impact – an openly known supernatural-certified attorney."

"Comforting," Camille said dryly.

She looked at the photo again, at the club's door, at the faint suggestion of people standing in shadow just beyond the frame. Someone had owned that doorway. Someone had stood there night after night, deciding who got to enter, who got to drink, who got protection from whatever law was hunting them.

Someone had probably thought they could borrow power without paying.

"What are you really showing me?" Camille asked.

"That this—" Mireille tapped the marks on Camille's forearm, "—is not a local phenomenon. It's not about the LeBlancs. It's not about you. It's older and bigger and it will keep finding people in every era who think they can slip between the cracks."

"Good," Camille said. "Maybe it'll scare them sooner next time."

"Maybe," Mireille said. "Or maybe they'll make the same mistakes you did. Different clothes, different laws, same hunger."

Camille folded the clipping and slipped it back into the folder, then pushed it toward Mireille. "Keep it. It belongs in your archive."

"It belongs in ours," Mireille said. "You're part of this now. You don't have to touch the current directly to help keep its books."

Camille thought of Isabelle's boxes of documents, stacked knee-high in her living room—the lawsuit they were building against Belle Rive's holding company, the clean-up orders, the medical records. All the paper weight of a house finally being forced to pay what it owed.

"I'm starting with home," Camille said. "Belle Rive. The LeBlanc corporations. The pro bono work I should have been doing ten years ago."

"And after that?" Mireille asked.

Camille considered the question. The rain eased, shifting from a downpour to a steady patter.

"After that, I'll take the cases the current won't let me walk past," she said. "The ones that feel… wrong when I try to ignore them."

"An ethical barometer with teeth," Mireille said. "I approve."

She stood, gathering the folder and the empty containers. At the doorway, she paused.

"Do you want to see the rest of the clippings?" Mireille asked. "New York, Chicago, some town out West whose name I can never remember. People like you. People like me."

"Not yet," Camille said. "If I start collecting ghosts from other cities before I finish with my own, I'll never sleep again."

"You assume you're meant to sleep much," Mireille said, amused. "That's adorable. For now, I'll leave them here with you, just in case you find yourself not sleeping and opt for a little late-night light reading."

Mireille left with a wink and the faint scent of incense trailing behind her.

The apartment felt quiet after she was gone. Not empty—Camille was learning to distinguish the difference. The current didn't make places empty. It filled them with memory until you learned how to live alongside it.

She cleared the table, rinsed the bowls, folded the bar committee's decision and set it in a plain folder in her desk. No framing. No display.

Her license was no longer a trophy. It was a weapon she'd have to handle carefully.

On her way back to the living room, she paused by the small bookshelf she'd started two weeks earlier—a new section, separate from her case law and legal texts. On it sat a row of black binders, each labeled in her precise handwriting.

CORRECTIONS — DURANT CASES (REVIEWED)

LEBLANC LITIGATION — ISABELLE

One thin spine at the end, newly added:

OTHER CURRENTS — HISTORICAL

That last binder held only three things so far.

A photocopy of the Leda's article.

A handwritten note from Émiline with a case citation from 1974 that "smelled wrong."

And a blank sheet of paper, labeled at the top: Working Principles. A place to write rules she hadn't fully articulated yet.

She opened the binder, added one more line beneath the heading.

1. No outcome is worth more than the truth required to get it.

Her pen hovered. Then:

2. No correction without accounting for all who will be harmed by it.

She closed the binder and slid it back into place.

Outside, the rain stopped. Sun broke weakly through the clouds, turning the wet street into a mirror. In the window glass, Camille caught her reflection—same bones, same eyes, new marks. The woman who'd walked into Belle Rive for a weekend of power games would not have recognized this version of herself.

Good.

Her phone buzzed on the table. A new email, subject line:

> INQUIRY: POST-CONVICTION ASSISTANCE
> (RE: 1998 ARSON CASE)

The body was brief. A woman writing on behalf of her brother, imprisoned for nearly thirty years on an arson charge he'd always claimed was "too convenient." She'd seen Camille's name in a story about "occult corruption" of trials and wanted to know if Camille "helped people on the other side, too."

Camille felt the familiar stir at the base of her spine. The current's attention. Not a shove, not a pull—more like a raised eyebrow.

She typed:

> *I don't promise outcomes. I promise the truth. If that's what you want, we can talk.*

She hit send.

For a moment, she stood in the doorway, listening to the city, to the quiet hum of the refrigerator, to the internal echo of water over stone.

Somewhere, in another city, in another decade, someone else would be standing in a doorway like this. A woman in a beaded dress with smoke in her hair. A bartender with a ledger behind the bar. A speakeasy owner looking at a crooked set of scales chalked on a back door, wondering when the bill would come due.

It would.

She picked up her bag, her keys, and the slim black notebook she now carried everywhere. On the first page, in neat handwriting, she'd written:

DURANT & CO. — OUTCOMES, HONESTLY
OBTAINED.

It wasn't a firm name yet. It might never be.

But it was a start.

Camille turned off the lights, locked the door, and stepped out
into the bright, wet evening.

The air smelled of asphalt and magnolia and, faintly, river. The
current moved beneath the city's skin, restless and patient and
endlessly precise.

For the first time since she'd passed the bar, Camille Durant was
exactly what she told people she was.

She walked toward her next appointment, feeling its attention
on her—not as a threat now, but as a witness. And as she
adjusted the file in her hand, the newsprint photo fell out. As
she reached down to pick it up, something caught her eye in the
picture. It was another old photo from the 1920s burned-out
Chicago club. But this one was different. In this photo, if you
squinted, the set of chalked scales seemed to tilt one fraction
closer to being level.

About the Author

C.L. Carmichael

Chicago-native turned Tampa Bay transplant, C.L. Carmichael is an avid reader a lifelong fan of Anne Rice, J.R.R. Tolkien and works that blur the line between the supernatural and reality.

Her stint as a legal assistant early in life sparked her fascination with contracts' fine print—where the devil hides in the details—lending fuel for "The Belle Rive Ledger," her debut supernatural thriller where justice bites back.

She crafts unbreakable women navigating cutthroat worlds and rewriting the rules. Balancing of the Scales of Justice begins.

www.ingramcontent.com/pod-product-compliance
Lightning Source LLC
Chambersburg PA
CBHW061425150726
47987CB00001B/102